A CHOOSE YOUR PATH HOCKEY BOOK

by

Lisa M. Bolt Simons

Minneapolis, Minnesota

# Dedication

To Anthony S., thanks for setting me straight on all things hockey.


# Acknowledgements

Thank you to Mike B. for your insight into being a hockey goalie.

Edited by Ryan Jacobson
Game design and "How to Use This Book" by Ryan Jacobson
Cover art by Stephen Morrow

Author photo by Jillian Raye Photography. The following images used under license from Shutterstock.com: Bardocz Peter (hockey rink), Michael Pettigrew (promotional photograph), MSF (hockey player), and VitaminCo (hockey stick)

10 9 8 7 6 5 4 3 2 1





Published by Lake 7 Creative, LLC
Minneapolis, MN 55412
www.lake7creative.com





Printed in the U.S.A.

ISBN: 978-1-940647-22-7; eISBN: 978-1-940647-23-4

# Table of Contents

# How to Use This Book

As you read *Save the Season!*, your goal is simple: make it to the happy ending on page 156. It's not as easy as it sounds. You will sometimes be asked to jump to a distant page. Please follow these instructions. Sometimes you will be asked to choose between two or more options. Decide which you feel is best, and go to the corresponding page. (Be careful; some options will lead to disaster.) Finally, if a page offers no instructions or choices, simply continue to the next page.

## EARN POINTS

Along the way, you will sometimes collect points for your decisions. Points are awarded for

A) confidence,
B) skill,
C) speed, and
D) teamwork.

Keep track of your points using a bookmark that you can cut out on page 159 (or on a separate piece of paper). You'll need the points later on.

## TALENT SCORE

Before you begin, you must determine your talent score. This number stands for the natural ability that your character, Adam, was born with. You can get your talent score in one of three ways:

*Quick Way*: Give yourself a talent score of two.

*Standard Way*: If you have any dice, roll one die. The number that you roll is your talent score. (You only get one try. So if you roll a one, you're stuck with it.)

*Fun Way*: Get a parent or guardian's help (to make sure you're in a safe place where no one—and nothing—can be hurt or damaged). Turn an empty garbage can onto its side so that the opening is on the floor, facing you. Stand six steps away. With a broom, gently try to swat a crumpled ball of paper into the garbage can. Take six tries. Every time you swat the paper into the can, you get a point. You only get six swings, whether you hit the paper or not. If you miss all six, that's okay. As long as you're a good sport and don't get mad, give yourself one talent point for trying the *Fun Way*. Give yourself one skill point, too. After all, skill gets better with practice.

# Your Starting Team

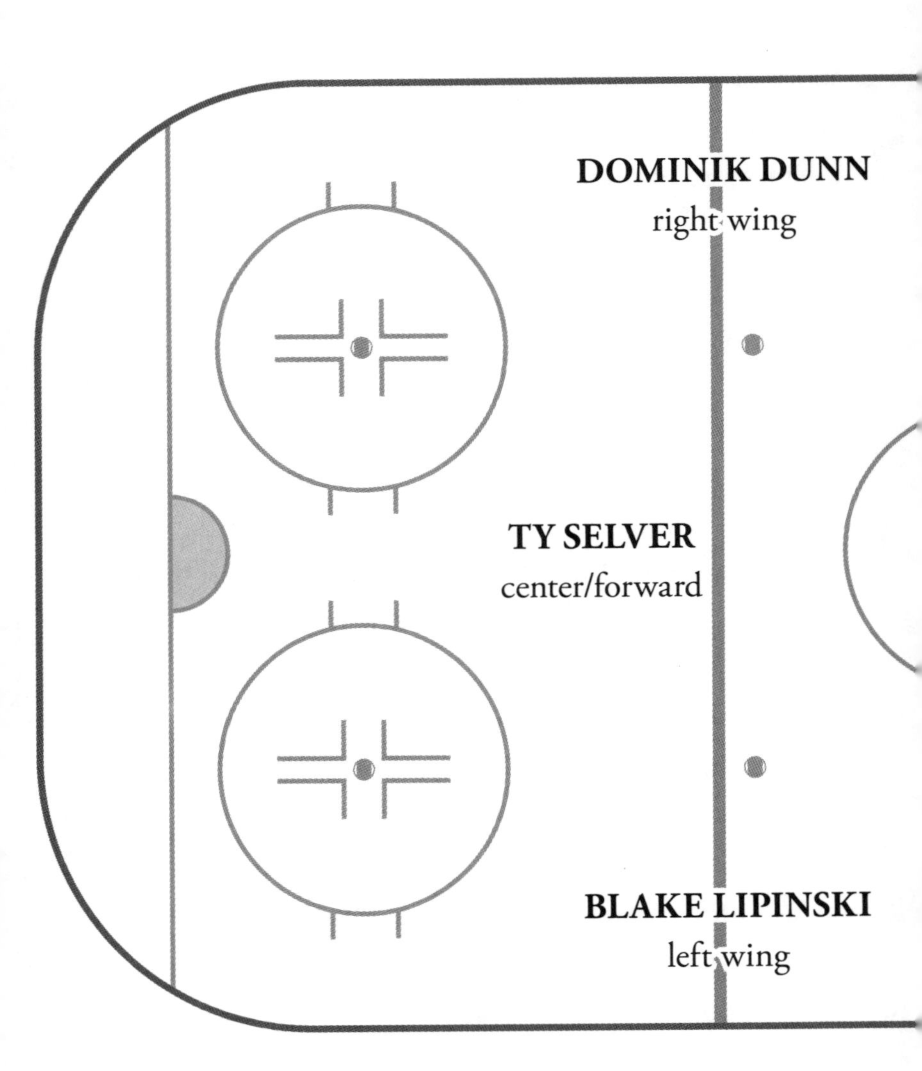

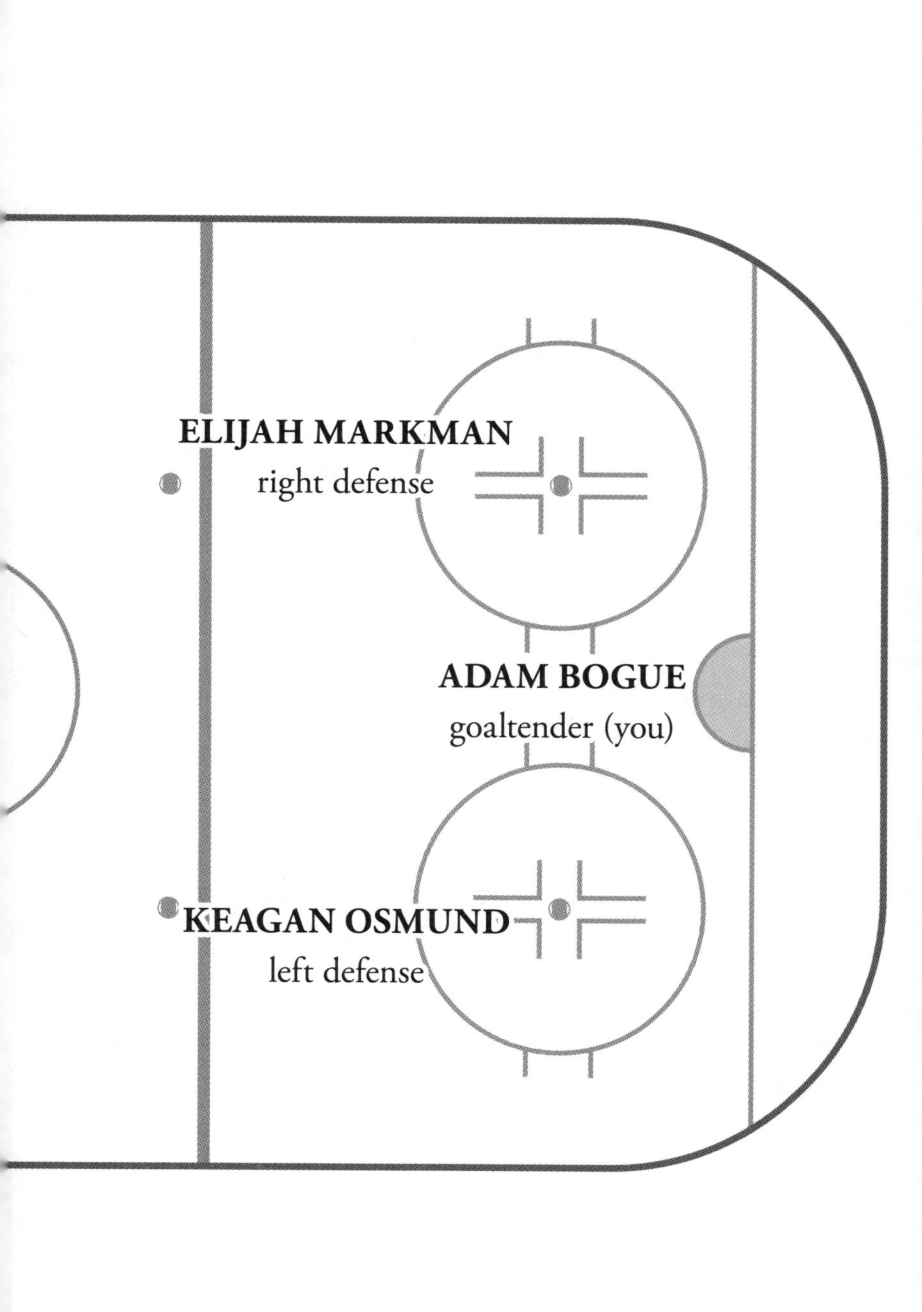
ELIJAH MARKMAN
right defense
ADAM BOGUE
goaltender (you)
KEAGAN OSMUND
left defense

# Prologue

*Author's note: Do you have your talent points yet? If not, please read pages 4–5.*

Your sister is playing like she's on fire, which is ironic because it's 18 degrees at the outdoor hockey rink. Tiny fluffs of snow fall onto the ice, making it almost perfect weather for a neighborhood pickup game.

At one end of the ice, Anna—your twin sister—guards the goal. So far, she's stopped every shot against her. You're at the other end of the ice, playing goalie for your team—and you're struggling. You keep slipping, dropping too quickly, and rebounding shots to the other team. In fact, you and your friends are losing by a score of 0–4.

Five minutes later, it's 0–6.

Every time you see Anna stop a goal, you want to scream. It's like she can't make a mistake.

Your mood isn't helped by Ty Selver, a forward on her team who keeps scoring against you. He always acts like he's better than everyone else, and each of his four goals only makes it worse.

One of your best friends, Billy VonRuden, is on her team tonight, too. He's one of the best players around. That just makes her team look even better.

Speaking of Billy, at the other end of the ice, Anna leans over and whispers into his ear. He listens, and he smiles. Then he zooms toward you with the puck.

You get into position, silently trying to answer two questions at the same time: What did she say to him, and where will he take his shot?

For a moment, you think that maybe he'll pass it to Ty. On the other hand, Billy's favorite shot is the five hole—the open space between your legs—because his shot is so quick. Should you play against the pass, or will you concentrate on protecting the five hole? What will you choose to do?

To defend the pass, go to page 40.

To guard the five hole, go to page 22.

It might be easier to tell Mr. Bogs that all is well, but you decide to give him the truth—even with Anna right next to you.

"To be honest, it's kind of tough this year," you say. "Anna is another one of the goalies."

**AWARD YOURSELF 1 CONFIDENCE POINT.**

You expect Anna to get upset, but she only adds a comment. "Our girls' program got too small, so they canned it."

Mr. Bogs nods. "I guess I don't understand what the problem is. You're still playing, right?" he asks you.

"The problem is that I've been playing all the games, and Anna doesn't like it."

"My version of the story," Anna says, "is that our coach won't play me because I'm a girl."

"Oh, that's not good," Mr. Bogs agrees.

Anna looks at you. "No, it's not good."

"But isn't that illegal or against the rules?" your teacher asks. He probably already knows the answer.

"He won't admit it," says Anna. "He'll just say Adam and Kohl are better goalies."

"Wow. I wish I could do something. You probably need to talk to your parents about it."

"Yeah, I really do," Anna agrees.

"Oh, great," you say—and then you regret it.

"What? Are you worried Mom and Dad will pull you off the team?" asks Anna.

"No, I'm worried about you ticking off the other players even more."

"No, you're just worried about *you*."

Mr. Bogs holds up his hands. "Okay, twin wonders, that will do. I don't want to be a ref here when I know nothing about it." He walks over to his desk and writes out passes. "Here you go."

Even at practice, you can't get the conversation with Anna out of your head. You try to put yourself in her place. What if you were the only guy on a girls' team and the coach wouldn't play you?

You study her in the crease. She really does have skill. But why is that? It's almost as if she really, truly is better than you. Almost.

# 6

# Bad Decisions

Today is the fifth game of the season. Your record is 2–2. Your team is playing the Summit Colts at home. The Colts have been an even matchup since you started playing hockey. The wins and losses are about half and half, so no one ever knows who will win. It's not like playing the Moylan Muskies, when your team always wins, or the Rice Lake Grizzlies, when you always lose.

Over the past week, it's become obvious that your sister and Ty definitely *like* each other. They talk before practice, during practice (when Coach isn't watching), and after practice. They talk at school. They talk on the phone. You honestly can't believe it. The meanest guy you know. She should *like* Elijah, instead. He's a super nice guy.

After warming up, you skate to the crease and chew up the ice. You really want to win this game.

The first period, you hold the Colts out of the net. The other goalie does the same. No score. That's okay. You'd rather tie than lose.

In the second period, a Colt shoots from the blue line. There are too many players in front of you, so you don't see the shot. The puck slides right past you. Goal.

You angrily hit the pipes with your stick as the arena announcer says the name of the player who scored.

During the intermission, Coach isn't as harsh as he sometimes gets. "Tighten up. Be more aggressive at the Colts' net. Defend Adam better. Not bad overall, though," he says.

The third period is different. It's as if Summit was replaced by an Olympic team. The shots keep coming, and three of them go in.

Down 1–4, you look toward the bench to see if the coach is going to pull you out of the game. He doesn't even look your way.

*Okay, keep playing.*

After goal number five flies over your shoulder, you hear Anna yell, "Keep your eye on the puck!"

When number six lifts above your leg and under your arm, you kind of want to throw up.

There are less than four minutes to play, and the Blizzard are down by five goals. This game is out of hand. Maybe now's a chance for Anna to get some time in the crease. You could ask Coach to put her in. However, you don't want to look like a quitter. Perhaps you should just stay in the game and finish it? What will you choose to do?

To ask Coach to play Anna, go to page 30.

To stay in the game, go to page 66.

You can practically hear your mom talking inside your head: *You're Anna's twin brother. That means your connection is tight—for the rest of your lives.*

You always pretend to gag when she says that, but it's true. After hockey is over, you'll still be twins. You have to say something to her. She'd do it for you.

You follow her down the hallway. Anna sits on the floor with her back against the wall, her head bowed and held between her hands.

You crouch down. "Hey, Zantana," you say.

You're the only one who gets away with using that nickname. As you two grew up and learned to rhyme, "Zantana" was the word you rhymed with "Anna," and the nickname stuck. It was funny when you two were little. But, now, when her friends call her that, she punches them in the arm.

You continue, "This whole thing stinks, I know—"

"Go away, Adam. You're not helping."

"Okay, listen. If you were on the girls' team, you'd be competing against Lauren Hanegraaf. I bet she'd be the number one goalie."

Anna looks at you, her nose crinkled. "Thanks a lot," she says sarcastically.

You shrug. "Sorry, I just mean your situation isn't all that different. Or, rather, it is and it isn't. You know?"

Anna looks down at the floor. "Yeah, I guess you're right," she mumbles. "It's probably a good thing she moved, or I wouldn't have a spot on the team at all."

No one says anything for a moment.

"I wish we'd move, so I could play with other girls," Anna says, at last. "I don't get why there were so many before, and now the whole team is pretty much gone."

"Our season is just starting," you say. "Let's take it one practice at a time. Okay?"

Anna doesn't respond.

You stand. "Come on. Mom's picking us up."

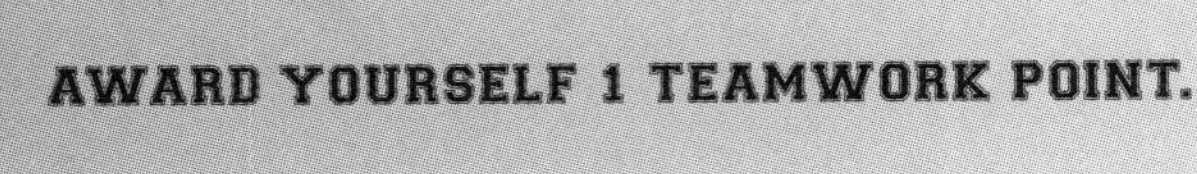


**Go to the next page.**

It's a good thing that your mom drives a Suburban, so you and your sister can both throw your huge bags of hockey gear into the trunk. You get into the front seat, Anna in back. Normally, she'd argue about who gets to sit where. But today she probably wants to skip the chit-chat. Your hunch is confirmed when she puts on her headphones and closes her eyes.

"How was practice?" your mom asks.

It went well for you, so you can tell Mom that. But should you also tell her about Anna? Your sister tends to keep things to herself, so she'll be mad if you "tattle," as she calls it. But your mom would want to know about Anna. That means you can either do what your sister would want or what your mom would want. What will you choose to do?

To tell Mom about Anna, go to page 52.

To talk only about your day, go to page 46.

"Let me make this perfectly clear," continues Coach. "We're going to run our plays, we're going to skate hard, and we're going to—"

You stand and move toward the door that Anna just exited. Coach stops talking and stares at you.

"What are you doing, Bogue?" he asks.

"I need to check on my sister."

He shakes his head. "She's a big girl. She can handle herself. You need to let me finish talking."

"Sorry, Coach, that's my sister."

You hear him start to speak again, but you don't wait around to listen. You open the door and quickly follow Anna down the hall.

She skirts through the foyer where the parents are hanging out before the game. She keeps going until she gets to the rink door that leads to the Blizzard's bench. She enters, letting it close behind her.

When you go in, Anna is hunched over with her head in her hands

"Hey," you say. What more would she want to hear? "Don't pay attention to the coach. I know this stinks, but . . ." you pause. "Listen: It's hard not to let this stuff get to you. But if you can't sit there and take it, you're never going to play."

"I don't care," she mutters.

"You've been at all the practices. You work hard. Coach will see it, soon enough, and get you in."

She looks at you. "Adam, you don't even want me in. Why are you saying all this?"

"You're a good goalie."

She shakes her head and turns away from you, just as the Blizzard take the ice.

"We should get out there," you say. "We should skate with our team." When Anna doesn't answer, you start toward the ice without her.

Coach barges into the bench area and stops you. "I'm glad you're both here. I hope you had a nice chat because I have news that affects you both. Anna, you're my number two goalie now. You just might see the ice this season, after all."

You slap her on the shoulder. "See, Anna? I told you. That's great news!"

"Wipe that smile off your face, Bogue. She's number two because you're number three. You walked out while I was talking. That tells me you're not a team player. You won't get minutes on the ice again."

**Go to page 81.**

You have to stick up for Anna. She's your sister. But you're nervous. *Deep breath.*

"Guys, stop slamming Anna," you say. "She holds her own out there."

Ty stops unlacing his skate, and he sits up straight. "What did you say, Bogue?"

"I said stop knocking down Anna.'"

"Why?" Ty answers. "I know you rip her, too. She's your backup. If you mess up, she might become our new starting goalie." He looks over at Kohl. "Sorry, dude, but it's true."

Kohl shrugs and keeps taking off his pads.

None of the other players talk to you after that. But they don't really talk to Ty either. At least everyone has stopped making fun of Anna.

**AWARD YOURSELF 1 TEAMWORK POINT.**

You and your sister ignore each other in the car and at home. You both eat dinner and answer your mom's questions in two words or less.

Finally, your dad breaks the sound of chewing and swallowing. "Okay, you two, what's up?"

"Nothing," you both say.

"I don't believe you," he replies.

"I'm just tired," says Anna.

"Yeah, me, too," you add.

"And I'm nervous about our first game," says Anna.

"Yeah, me, too," you say again.

Your mom nods. "I was always nervous before my volleyball games."

Dad says, "Same with me, before swim meets."

"Do you know the time I was most nervous?" your mom asks. "It was against our rival, Air Academy. I couldn't . . ."

You stop listening to her story. You want to finish your dinner and go to your room. You feel like a stick wrapped tightly by tape, too tightly, suffocating.

**Go to page 59.**

No, Billy won't pass. It's a pickup game, just for fun, something all of you have done together for years. These games settle into memory. They're all about great plays, who outdid whom, and neighborhood bragging rights.

You squat slightly, preparing for the low shot. When Billy's close enough, he swings his stick. You drop down to the ice, and . . .

. . . the puck soars up, over your left glove, straight into the net.

Now, you know *exactly* what your sister told him: "His weakness is that he holds his glove hand too low." She's right, and Billy proved it—although after all of these years, he probably already knows your weakness. Anna just made sure of it.

"Good try," Billy says over his shoulder as he skates toward center ice.

"Whatever," you mumble.

You've had enough, and you want to go home. But you don't want your friends to give you a hard time or to call you a "quitter." Actually, it wouldn't even be your friends as much as Ty Selver. He's had a bad attitude since back when you two started Mini Mites.

The only kid who has ever gotten along with him is Keagan Osmund. But in these pickup games, you're stuck with whomever shows up. It's always better when only one of them comes. It's always *best* when neither of them does.

Tonight, you only have to worry about Ty—but he's enough. Of course, you need to get used to dealing with both of them again. The new season starts tomorrow, and they're both on your team.

You're the Lakeside Bay Blizzard's starting goalie—and you guys have a chance to be great this year. Hopefully, you'll play better than this. You're not sure when Anna got to be so good. But tonight, you're off your game and she is 100% on.

Oh, well, just forget about her great game. The real hockey season begins tomorrow. Ty and Keagan aside, you can't wait for it.

# 1

# Two Goalies

Your name is Adam Jeffrey Bogue. You live with your family in the small town of Lakeside Bay. One of the most awesome things about living here is the number of lakes. More precisely, it's the water in the lakes that freezes every winter. You never have to worry about finding ice to skate on.

You can't remember a time when you didn't skate, although your parents say you first put on skates when you were almost three. Your dad loves telling the story of how you didn't fall once—you just kept inching ahead, eyes up and focused. You weren't scared one bit.

Now, all of these years later, you're eating dinner at home with your parents and Anna. As you shovel in the lasagna—you're always hungry after a hard practice—your mom asks how hockey went today.

"Fine," you say between chews.

"Awesome!" Anna says.

"So it's okay being with boys?" Mom asks her.

"I don't have a choice," she answers.

Mom shrugs. "I know, but do you think it will be weird all season?"

"Maybe," says Anna. "I played with my friends for so long. But . . . today was kind of cool."

"It's really too bad that Shae Beaupre and Maddie McDonough moved, and so many other girls quit. At least the boys' team will let you play." Your mom turns to you. "Isn't this a nice opportunity for Anna? We're so glad she can still be on a team."

You chew your garlic bread as slowly as possible. Your parents stare at you relentlessly, waiting for an answer.

"We're both goalies, Mom," you finally say.

"There are always backup goalies, though. Right, Adam?" asks your dad. Even with two kids in hockey, he still doesn't know the rules very well. He was a swimmer in high school and college—he never played hockey.

Now, you have to answer. The truth is you absolutely do *not* want your sister as your backup. You don't care that there isn't a girls' team. You worked hard for years to become a starting goalie.

However, if you tell your family that, you'll hurt Anna's feelings. But maybe your parents will put a stop to this—so you can actually *enjoy* your hockey season. On the other hand, you have a good sense of humor; you crack people up all the time. So you could make a joke. It won't change anything, but at least your sister's feelings will be spared.

You have to decide how to answer your dad. What will you choose to do?

To tell the truth, go to page 54.

To make a joke, go to page 35.

There's nothing you can do to make your sister feel better. Besides, if you leave now, Coach might bench you for the game—or the whole season.

The coach finishes his pep talk. "Okay," he ends, "it's almost time to get out there. Take a few minutes and get yourselves ready."

Ty leaves the locker room. *What is he doing?* Maybe he wants to bug your sister. You have to follow him.

When you get to the hallway, you see him walk through the rink door. You hurry to the door. But when you open it, he comes back through.

"Watch it, Bogue," he hisses.

You look into the rink. Anna is already sitting on the bench. You can't get to her from here. Neither could Ty. Again, you wonder, *What is he doing?*

You turn and follow him back down the hallway. He passes the locker room and leads you through the foyer full of parents.

"Hi, Adam," says Blake Lipinski's mom.

You feel bad for not stopping, since you've known her all of your life. You wave a quick hello and continue after Ty.

You reach the door that leads to the Blizzard's bench. When you open it, Anna is hunched over with her head in her hands. Ty is leaning in close to her.

"Leave Anna alone," you tell him.

He looks up and glares at you. "Do you mind? I happen to be *talking* to your sister."

"Anna," you say, ignoring him, "are you okay?"

She looks at you as if she wants to take her blocker glove and shove it down your throat.

"You're okay?" you ask again.

She barely nods her head.

You go back out the door as your team gets onto the ice. You run as fast as you can back to the locker room for your stick. You're quite adept at running in pads and skates. The pads are like extra body parts you've had years to get used to. The skates are like your second feet.

On the way, you wonder, *Why would Anna be talking to Ty?* It always seems as if he hates her, and now he's consoling her.

**Go to the next page.**

When you get back to the locker room, you see Ty's stick there, too. It's about time for the joke to be on him for a change—and this is a perfect opportunity for a prank. You could hide his stick; that would be a good signal for him to leave Anna alone. Or maybe you should just let Anna deal with him. In that case, you could bring his stick to him as he hurries to the ice. What will you choose to do?

To hide Ty's stick, go to page 78.

To bring Ty his stick, go to page 70.

You make up your mind. It's time to let Anna show her stuff. When the referee blows the whistle, you skate to the bench.

"Coach, I need out. I think you should put Anna in and see what she can do."

He stares at you for a moment. You try your hardest not to look away.

"There are only a few minutes left in the game," he says. "It certainly can't get any worse out there."

"I know," you say. "But I need a break. Give Anna a chance, okay?"

Coach looks at Anna. Then he looks back at you and shakes his head. "I can't believe this," he hisses. He points at Kohl. "You're in."

Anna turns away in anger. All you can do is sit on the bench with her.

In the locker room, the coach lambasts the team and then storms out. As soon as he's gone, Ty and Keagan—and a handful of others—start calling you "chicken." They cough it, whisper it, and even chant it.

You tried to do something nice for your sister, but they think you quit on them.

**Go to the next page.**

You're humiliated at each of the next two practices. Coach doesn't even let you onto the ice. Your job is to sit and watch while Kohl and Anna play goalie.

When your mom picks you and Anna up from the rink, you get into the backseat and don't say a word.

At home, you pull your mom and dad into the living room. "I quit hockey," you say.

"What?" Mom asks, sounding startled. "Why?"

"At the last game, I asked Coach to take me out. I was trying to give Anna a chance, but he and the whole team think I just gave up on them." Tears form in the corners of your eyes. You quickly wipe them away.

"Adam," your dad says, "you can't quit. You'll regret it for the rest of your life."

"No, I'll regret going back there, day after day. I'll regret being picked on and embarrassed for nothing—because Coach made it clear: I'm never getting on the ice for him again!"

You stomp away from your parents before they can respond. As you hurry toward your bedroom, you shout over your shoulder, "My mind is made up. I quit!"

**Go to page 81.**

You really don't feel like talking about Anna and the goalie drama right now. So why not tell him what he wants to hear?

"Hockey is awesome," you say with as much fake joy as you can muster.

**AWARD YOURSELF 1 TEAMWORK POINT.**

"That's great news," replies Mr. Bogs with a big grin. "What about your season, Anna?"

She lets out a deep exhale, like she's been holding her breath since the season began. "It's really bad."

Mr. Bogs' smile drops. You close your eyes to keep from rolling them.

"Really? Why?" he asks.

"I'm a goalie who doesn't play," says Anna.

"Yes, I can see how that would be bad."

"It's worse than it sounds," she continues. "Our girls' hockey program got too small, so they canned it."

You decide to speak up. "Her problem is that I've been playing all the games, and Anna doesn't like it."

"My version of the story," Anna says, "is that our coach won't play me because I'm a girl."

"Oh, that's not good," Mr. Bogs agrees.

Anna looks at you. "No, it's not."

"But isn't that illegal or against the rules or something?" your teacher asks. He probably already knows the answer.

"Coach won't admit it," says Anna. "He'll just say Adam and Kohl are better goalies."

"Wow. I wish I could do something. You probably need to talk to your parents about it."

"Yeah, I really do," Anna agrees.

"Oh, great," you say—and then you regret it.

"What? Are you worried Mom and Dad will pull you off the team?" asks Anna.

"No, I'm worried about you ticking off the other guys even more."

"No, you're just worried about *you*."

Mr. Bogs holds up his hands. "Okay, twin wonders, that'll do. I don't want to be a ref here when I know nothing about it." He walks over to his desk and writes out passes. "Here you go."

Even at practice, you can't get the conversation with Anna out of your head. You try to put yourself in her place. What if you were the only guy on a girls' team and the coach wouldn't play you?

You study her in the crease. She really does have skill. But why is that? It's almost as if she really, truly is better than you. Almost.

**Go to page 12.**

"No, Dad," you answer with a smile. "There are only backup goalies on Tuesdays."

Anna laughs so hard that milk squirts out her nose.

It causes you to laugh so much that you nearly fall out of your chair. "That was totally awesome," you say between gasps.

**AWARD YOURSELF 1 TEAMWORK POINT.**

Your mom mumbles, "Gross," while your dad goes into the kitchen. He comes back with a roll of paper towels for your sister.

"That hurt my nose and the back of my throat," Anna says, wiping up her mess. She looks at her plate. "And my lasagna is ruined."

"Not really," you note. "It's just what your stomach looks like: lasagna-and-milk casserole."

"Adam," your mom snaps, "I'm still trying to eat."

Your dad looks back and forth between you and your sister. "It's going to be an interesting season."

The smile falls off your face.

**Go to the next page.**

After the dishes are all washed, Anna starts on her English paper. You work on math. But your mind is on other things . . . like today's practice. Anna may be your twin sister, but she needs a lesson about who's stronger and better at hockey.

Besides, she deserves some mischief. She's always causing problems for you, yet you get in trouble way more than she does. It's probably because your mom tries to take it easy on her.

As for your plan, your best friend, Hudson, has been teaching you some wrestling moves. Hudson and his brother are two of the best wrestlers around.

You stand and peek into the kitchen. Mom is still in there. She definitely wouldn't approve of your idea. For that matter, you wonder why she doesn't understand that you and Anna sometimes have to razz each other. Your mom fought with her two sisters, growing up.

You tiptoe to the couch and sit down. "Hey, Anna, can you help me with this math problem?"

As much as you hate to admit it, Anna is a math whiz. Your teacher never tells you that Anna's smarter than you, but he doesn't have to.

Anna sighs and walks over. When she gets close, you throw your homework to the side and grab her. You take her to the ground and pin her arms.

She doesn't even yelp.

You tap her forehead. "Typewriter. Note to Anna: You are—"

Before you know what happens, she spins and flips you. Now, you're on the ground with *your* arms pinned.

Anna leans in close to your face. "Don't ever do that again." She stands and walks back to the table.

It's a good thing Hudson didn't see that. You'd never hear the end of it.

# 2

# Unfair Practices

It doesn't take many practices to see that your twin sister is a really good goalie. She's not as good as you, though. Is she? You both played hockey for so many years, but you also attended summer goalie camps to work on your skills. Plus, you used to play center and wing, so you know how to read the scorers.

As for Anna, she's always been a goalie—and sometimes a gymnast. You wonder if her time in gymnastics helps her to get down into the butterfly easier; she's way more flexible than you.

That's something you should work on: flexibility. You have to be better than Anna at everything. You won't let her steal your position away from you—not that it's likely to happen.

Coach Wheeler won't play her. In fact, after practice, you overhear him telling her that. "It's a boys' hockey team, Anna," he says.

"I'm just as good as Adam," she pleads. "And you're supposed to play me. The hockey association decided that when they said I could join the team."

"The association said I have to give you a uniform. They didn't say I have to play you. I get to start whoever I think will do the best job. So far, Adam's really been stepping up. End of discussion."

You hear Coach's office door slam shut. Then you hear Anna's voice echo in the hall. "I'm stepping up, too!"

She's frustrated. Maybe she's ready to give up. If she quits the team, then your troubles are over. Then again, she's your sister—and your teammate—whether you like it or not. Maybe you should go and offer some words of support. Will you go to her and console her? Or will you walk away and forget that you heard a thing? What will you choose to do?

To talk to Anna, go to page 15.

To leave Anna alone, go to page 42.

Billy will pass. It's a pickup game, just for fun, something all of you have done together for years. These games settle into memory. They're all about great plays, who outdid whom, and neighborhood bragging rights. Ty has a chance to score his fifth goal on you, and Billy wants to be a part of it.

You slide slightly to your right, preparing for the pass. To your surprise, Billy never gives up the puck. When he's close enough, he swings his stick, and . . .

. . . the puck soars up, over your left glove, straight into the net.

Now, you know *exactly* what your sister told him: "His weakness is that he holds his glove hand too low." She's right, and Billy proved it—although after all of these years, he probably already knows your weakness. Anna just made sure of it.

"Good try," Billy says over his shoulder as he skates toward center ice.

"Whatever," you mumble.

You've had enough, and you want to go home. But you don't want your friends to give you a hard time or to call you a "quitter." Actually, it wouldn't even be your friends as much as Ty Selver. He's had a bad attitude since back when you two started Mini Mites.

The only kid who has ever gotten along with him is Keagan Osmund. But in these pickup games, you're stuck with whomever shows up. It's always better when only one of them comes. It's always *best* when neither of them does.

Tonight, you only have to worry about Ty—but he's enough. Of course, you'd better get used to dealing with both of them again. The new season starts tomorrow, and they're both on your team.

You're the Lakeside Bay Blizzard's starting goalie—and you guys have a chance to be great this year. Hopefully, you'll play better than this. You're not sure when Anna got to be so good. But tonight, you're off your game and she is 100% on.

Oh, well, just forget about her night. The real hockey season begins tomorrow. Ty and Keagan aside, you can't wait for it.

**Go to page 24.**

Anna is your competition, whether she's your sister or not. You should try to separate the sibling part from the competitor part. If your competition were sitting on the ground, would you go to him or her? Would you say that everything will be okay? No chance.

When it comes to playing goalie, Anna is not on your side. She's on her own side. So the right thing to do is to leave her be.

You walk into the lobby and pull out your cell phone. You call your mom and ask her to get to the arena as soon as she can.

**Go to page 17.**

In the third period, you do stop Falcon from scoring any goals. Ty ties the game with five minutes left to play. You wish it had been Billy or Dominik or Blake. Anyone but Ty.

The period ends, and the game goes into overtime. Three minutes into it, Dalton lifts the puck just over the goalie's left shoulder, and the Blizzard win, 4–3.

The victory doesn't seem to matter to Coach. He rips your play in front of the whole team. "What were you doing out there? That was a complete lack of focus. I mean, come on!"

You just stare at the locker room floor.

Anna approaches you after Coach leaves. The last thing you want is to talk to her. But by looking at her face, you know that she isn't going to give you a hard time. She's probably feeling lucky that it wasn't her who stunk so much. But, then, would she have given up three goals? Would she even have given up one?

"Hey," you say.

Anna pats your shoulder. "I don't care what Coach says. You played a good game."

"I let three shots go in."

"So? You stopped about 20 others."

You shrug. The coach wasn't impressed. You're not sure why she is.

"It was a good first game," she says.

"I bet you think you could've done better."

"What? Adam, I wasn't going to say that."

"You were thinking it," you reply.

"You have no idea what I was thinking."

You can't help it. Between feeling down and getting yelled at by your coach, the word just comes out: "Liar."

Anna's mouth drops open. She spins away from you and stomps down the hall.

When you get in the car, you don't speak to each other. In fact, two days go by without a word, not at home, school, or practice. Your parents, surprisingly, don't try to make you talk it out. At least, not now.

As if her anger is driving her skill, Anna seems to play better than ever. It's like she knows where the shots are going to go. You remember a quote by hockey legend Wayne Gretzky: "A good hockey player plays where the puck is. A *great* hockey player plays where the puck is going to be."

* * *

After some tough practices, the day of your first home game—against Moose Creek—arrives. Just a few minutes before it's time to skate onto the ice, Anna joins the team in the locker room. Ty leans in toward Keagan and whispers something. Both of them look at her and laugh.

"All right," Coach says, "Moose Creek is a team we can beat. Billy and Ty, keep our plays in those brains of yours. Alex, Elijah, and Keagan, do a better job of defending the net. Adam, I want you to improve your defense tonight, too. Anna, you're not going to play."

Anna's shoulders slump as the coach keeps talking. After a moment, she turns and opens the door so hard that it hits the wall.

The coach stops speaking for a second. But when the door closes, he starts again as if nothing happened. Will you stay in the locker room and listen to him? Or should you go after your sister? What will you choose to do?

To stay in the locker room, go to page 27.

To follow Anna, go to page 18.

Anna can speak for herself. If she wants to tell Mom what's going on, she will.

"Oh, it was fine. I decided to quit hockey and will now be teaching the fine art of booger weaving."

"That's disgusting, Adam," your mom says. But she smiles. "How did practice really go?"

"Good," you say. You look back at Anna, then add, "At least, for me it did."

Your mom looks into the rearview mirror, shakes her head slightly, then focuses back on the road.

When she parks the car in the garage, you get your equipment out to dry, so the skates don't rust. Drying the gear also airs out the sweat. You've heard some other parents complain about the stench of hockey equipment, but you've never noticed.

You try to help Anna with her stuff, too, but she doesn't look at you once.

**AWARD YOURSELF 1 TEAMWORK POINT.**

**Go to the next page.**

While your mom makes dinner, you work on math and Anna on science. You remember the first day of class, when the science teacher, Mr. Bogs, sat you two together. He said that he reserved front and center for twins. Then he let everyone else sit wherever they wanted.

Even though you sit beside her, it's as if you don't even know each other. You barely talk at school, in class or out. At practice, too. A few of the other guys talk to her, but not many. Some of them, especially Ty Selver, don't want her on the ice at all.

# 3

# Mean Boys

In practice, the whole team skates around the rink to get loose. Then the team stretches. After that, the team warms up the three goalies by shooting pucks at you, Anna, and Kohl Anderson. You really like seeing the shots coming at you, stopping them with all of your body. Even when you're not in the goal, you watch the other two, analyzing why they save certain shots and why they miss some, too.

Other drills include the Saint Cloud three-on-two, 15–10 fink, four-corner blue line drill, and wild passing, all to get your team ready for the upcoming season.

Practice usually ends with a small-area game. The rink gets split into thirds, and each goalie is assigned a chunk to protect.

Day in and day out, you have to admit it: Anna dominates. You always do well, too. Kohl, however, is a distant third.

Today, Coach Wheeler closes out practice by letting each player choose what to work on. For the goalies, he suggests either skating drills or more work in front of the net. What will you choose to do?

To try the skating drills, go to page 76.

To practice in the net, go to page 77.

Coach Wheeler calls everyone over. "Good practice today," he says. "First game is Saturday. I want you guys to be eating healthy and getting good sleep. Tomorrow, practice is at 6:15."

You skate to Locker Room 1. Anna goes to Locker Room 2, since she can't change with the guys. You often wonder if it's weird to be all by herself. Probably. She was close with all the girls on her old team.

When you walk into your locker room, you hear, "—when I scored that last goal on her? She's awful."

You look at Ty, taking off his elbow pads. He adds, "She needs to quit. We'll be laughed off the ice if she gets to play." He looks right at you, practically daring you to say something.

"I scored against her four straight times," Keagan Osmund says.

"I didn't score even once," Blake Lipinski admits.

"That's because your grandma outshoots you," Ty replies, and the boys all laugh.

**Go to the next page.**

Ty is always the one to stir things up. Of course, Anna can't defend herself because she doesn't hear what he and the others say. Should you stick up for your sister, since she can't? Or should you agree with them—at least about her needing to quit? It's important for a goalie to get along with his teammates. What will you choose to do?

To stick up for Anna, go to page 20.

To agree with them, go to page 58.

It's probably easier for you to talk right now than for your sister. Mom deserves to know what happened.

You quietly say, "Anna got mad that she isn't getting enough net time. Coach told her that he's playing the better goalie."

"He did not say you were *better*!" Anna shouts from the backseat.

Whoops, she was listening after all.

She continues, "He said he's playing the goalie who will do the best job."

"Same difference."

"No, it's not! He's playing you because you're a *boy* and better than Kohl Anderson."

"He never said that."

"Oh, be quiet," Anna snaps.

"Anna," your mom says, "that's enough. We'll talk about this later, in private."

The rest of the drive home is silent. You can tell that your mom is doing some major thinking. She's a social worker at the high school, so she has a lot of practice working on people's problems. You just wish she didn't practice her solutions on her own kids.

Anna stares out the window. You settle in and thank your lucky stars that you're the starting goalie. Part of you feels bad for your sister. The other part, a bigger part, is just glad you have the position that you've played all of your life.

When Mom parks the car in the garage, you get your equipment out to dry so that the skates don't rust. Drying the gear also airs out the sweat. You've heard other hockey parents complain about the stench of hockey equipment, but you've never noticed.

You try to help Anna with her stuff, too, but she pushes you out of the way.

"Quit talking for me!" she yells.

"I didn't think you'd want to tell Mom, so I did it for you. I was trying to be nice."

"That's for me to decide. Get out of my way." She pushes you again as she hurries into the house.

**AWARD YOURSELF 1 CONFIDENCE POINT.**

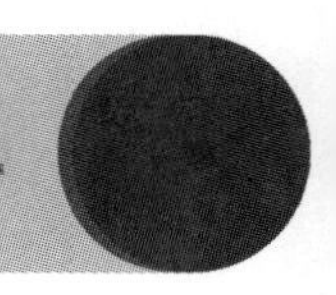

**Go to page 47.**

"Yes, Dad," you say. "Abby is a backup goalie. In case I get hurt."

"Or," Anna says, "in case Coach decides I'm better than you."

You stare at your sister as you swallow your next bite of lasagna. Then you say, "This is exactly why I don't want Anna on the team. It's *my* team. They're *my* friends. I've worked so hard for this!"

"And so has she," your mom answers. "No girls' team means she's on your team. That's just how it is."

"That's not fair to me. I don't want to play with her."

"That can be solved," your dad says, pointing his fork at you. "You don't have to be on the team. Your right to play doesn't trump her right to play."

You throw down your fork and push away from the table. You stand up, but your dad stops you in your tracks with a glare.

"Sit down," he says, "or you *will* be off the team, whether you like it or not."

You drop back into your chair, but you don't take another bite. You've lost your appetite.

**Go to page 36.**

You eat your chicken and think that you absolutely, positively cannot lose your position on the team. It's been too many years, too many practices, too many games. You can improve your grades, and you can do it without Anna's help.

**AWARD YOURSELF 1 CONFIDENCE POINT.**

You finish dinner and put your plate in the dishwasher. You grab your backpack and go upstairs to your room. You settle into your desk and crack open your science textbook.

The more you read, the more you understand. You get out the packet of questions that Mr. Bogs gave you and answer them all.

**Go to the next page.**

The next morning, Mr. Bogs keeps you and Anna after class. You imagine that he is what Santa Claus looked like in his twenties. He smiles all the time and has a deep belly laugh. He doesn't have a beard, but his eyes always seem mischievous . . . in a good way.

"The reason I'm keeping you after class is because I want to ask you how school is going."

"Good," Anna says.

"Fine," you reply.

"Are you sure, Adam? Your sister is getting an A, and you're getting a C. I only bring this up because I'm worried. Your parents told me at conferences that you have to keep your grades up in order to play sports."

"Yeah, so?"

"So you need to find a balance between sports and school. Someday, it'll be sports, school, and a job."

"I guess."

"Can Anna help you?" he asks.

"I did the questions last night," you say, "and I think I got them all."

Mr. Bogs smiles. "That's good to hear. So, then, how is hockey going?"

Good question. Of course, he wants you to say *good*, *great*, or *awesome*. You can tell him as much and put an end to the conversation—without opening up a bigger discussion. Or you can tell the truth: that it's hard to have fun this year because the other goalie—who just so happens to be Anna—is creating too much drama. Maybe saying so will lead to some happy solution. What will you choose to do?

To pretend everything is fine, go to page 32.

To tell the truth, go to page 10.

"Don't worry," you say. "Anna will quit before she ever gets to play."

You force a smile. *Anna is my competition. Anna is my competition.* The thought skates around and around in your mind. It doesn't make you feel better.

You and your sister ignore each other in the car and at home. You both eat dinner and answer your mom's questions in two words or less.

Finally, your dad breaks the sound of chewing and swallowing. "Okay, you two, what's up?"

"Nothing," you both say.

"I don't believe you," he replies.

"I'm just tired," says Anna.

"Yeah, me, too," you add.

"And I'm nervous about our first game," says Anna.

"Yeah, me, too," you say again.

Your mom nods. "I was always nervous before my volleyball games."

Dad says, "Same with me, before swim meets."

"Do you know the time I was most nervous?" your mom asks. "It was against our rival, Air Academy. I couldn't . . ."

You stop listening to her story. You want to finish your dinner and go to your room. You feel like a stick wrapped tightly by tape, too tightly, suffocating.

You finish eating and finally escape. You flop onto your bed, shut your eyes, and think . . .

*You lead the team onto the ice. You circle around with the others but soon get to your space on the rink: the crease in front of the net. You scrape the smooth parts of the ice with your skates in short motions, back and forth, moving from one end of the net to the other. It's called "chewing up the ice." Goalies do this for three big reasons:*

*One, smooth ice is bad for goalies. After all, you don't want to make a save and then slide away from the net because there's nothing to stop you.*

*Two, the Zambonis that clean and smooth out the ice always add extra water near the goals—since that's where most of the action is. There's not always time for the water to freeze between periods. By scraping the ice, you can turn that water into slush. Slush turns more quickly into ice, and it slows down the puck, which is way better for goalies. Water and pucks don't mix. For that matter, water and goalies don't mix either. You don't want to go down, get your equipment wet, and then have to stand there—wet and cold—for the rest of the game. You learned that lesson a few years ago. Never again.*

*Three, chewing up the ice gives you a burst of energy, a quick warm-up before play begins.*

You open your eyes, feeling more relaxed. You're not thinking of your sister. Not your parents. Not even your team. You know what to do out there on the ice. Just go out and do it.

# 4

# The First Game

Finally, the first game. It's in the town of Falcon, about an hour away. Your mom and dad offer to drive other players, too, so Elijah Markman and Dominik Dunn ride with you.

Anna sits in the far back with Elijah. He's one of the few teammates who's always nice to her. He never throws in any comments when Ty starts up. Now, they both play on their phones and ignore everything else.

You and Dominik don't say much, either. You don't feel like talking. Actually, you're so nervous that you feel more like throwing up with each mile.

You have so much to prove to your coach and team—especially since you worry that Anna could take your position from you. Although Coach says he won't play her, that could change quickly if the team loses. And even if he bypasses Anna, Coach could always put Kohl in the crease.

* * *

Most of the team stays pretty quiet while they get dressed. Even Ty. You guess they're all nervous, too.

You lead everyone onto the ice and circle around your half of the rink. Then you enter your space. You chew up the ice, tap the pipes on either side of the net with your stick, and practice your stance.

Your nerves fade. You feel ready.

Billy scores the first goal. Goal number two belongs to Dominik, assisted on a great pass by Billy. At the end of the first period, the Blizzard lead, 2–0.

When the second period starts, a Falcon forward gets off a perfect shot against you. It goes into the net through the five hole. You didn't get down fast enough.

Six minutes later, the same forward lifts the puck above your shoulder on your left. It should be an easy save, but you miss it completely. The score is 2–2.

Hockey is a team game, and you try to remind yourself of that. But you're the one who's supposed to stop the goals. If you don't stop them, your whole team loses. That's a lot of pressure. That's the life of a goalie.

With seven seconds left in the period, the very same Falcon forward scores his third goal against you: a hat trick for him. Part of you wishes that you could throw off your helmet and yell at all of your teammates for not defending the crease. Part of you wonders if this is nobody's fault but yours.

During the intermission, Coach does the yelling for you. "Defense, you need to step up!" Then he crouches next to you. "You can stop these goals, Adam."

You close your eyes and repeat his words: "You can stop these goals. You can stop these goals."

How many talent points do you have?

If you have three or more points, go to page 43.

If you have two or fewer points, go to page 82.

You eat your chicken and think that you absolutely, positively cannot lose your position on the team. It's been too many years, too many practices, too many games. You can improve your grades, but you can't do it without Anna's help. You guess you really don't have a choice.

You finish eating dinner and put your plate in the dishwasher. You take a deep breath and find Anna. She's lying on her bed, doing her science assignment.

"Good news," you say. "I have that homework, too. Don't you think it would be easier if we did it together?"

"No." She doesn't even look up.

"Let me ask again. Don't you think it would be easier if we did it together?"

"No." She still doesn't look up.

"When you teach someone, it's easier to understand."

She looks at you. "Adam, are you asking for help?" Her face lights up with a huge smile.

"Come on," you reply. "Don't make me say it."

She laughs. "Oh, yes, if you want help from me, you're going to say it." She must be enjoying this.

You sigh. "Fine. Anna, will you *please* help me?"

She sits up on the bed and gathers her work. "I'll work with you at the dining room table for half an hour." She walks out and strolls down the stairs.

This is not going to be fun.

You grab your backpack and follow her to the dining room. Anna sits at one end. You try to sit next to her, but she points at the other end. You set your stuff down and crack open your science textbook.

The more you read, the more you talk to Anna. And the more you talk to Anna, the more you understand. You get out the packet of questions that Mr. Bogs gave you, and, together, you answer them all.

**AWARD YOURSELF 1 TEAMWORK POINT.**

**Go to page 56.**

You're getting pummeled, but giving up the goalie position to Anna will only make you feel worse. Besides, you started this royal mess with your teammates. You should finish it with them, too.

Fortunately, you don't let any more goals in the net. You're relieved when the game ends, but you're nervous about how Coach is going to react. You're nervous about how your team will react, too.

As you shake hands with the Colts' players, the forward who scored a hat trick says, "You're terrible." That's never happened before: someone slamming you during a handshake. He caught you off guard, so you don't say a word before he skates away.

In the locker room, Coach glares at you. He yells more at the defensemen: Elijah, Alex, Brady, Keagan. Still, you let the goals in. You're to blame for the loss.

When the coach gets done dishing out his anger, he adds, "Get ready for an intense practice on Monday."

Anna walks over to you. "You messed up. Big time."

You gawk at her. "Do you think I don't know that?"

"Your form was off, your stance was off, and your decisions stunk."

"Get away from me," you snap.

She shakes her head and leaves.

She really grinds your gears. Does she think that she could've done better out there? Obviously, because her big mouth had to tell you how badly you did.

On your way out of the locker room, you notice Anna, but you don't see her bag of gear. She's chatting with her group of girlfriends, including a couple who quit hockey: Dominik's sister Mia and Billy's sister Avery. The other two, Chloe Kasper and Keely Sanborn, play basketball. At least *they* still have a girls' team for their sport.

You're angry at Anna, and sometimes your anger gets the better of you. You decide that she needs to be taught a lesson—and you know just what to do.

You put your gear against the wall in the lobby. Then, when no one is looking, you sneak into Locker Room 2. Anna's gear is packed in her bag. Why didn't she bring it out with her?

It doesn't matter, now. You take her shoulder pads, elbow pads, breezers, socks, and gloves. You scatter them under the shower heads. You decide not to touch the goalie pads; those are too expensive. Then you turn the showers on and run.

You sneak back to your bag and head for the door.

Your mom is just coming into the arena. "What is taking so long? I've been sitting out there, waiting."

"Sorry," you say. "Coach wanted to talk to me."

"Where's your sister?"

"Uh, over—uh, I don't know." You walk out the door, throw your gear into the back of the Suburban, and get in the front seat. You start to feel a little guilty about Anna's gear.

Your mom gets in, too. "Mia's mom is driving Anna." She puts the car in gear and starts for home.

You're glad that you live in a small town. It only takes about five minutes to get back to your house from the arena. Actually, you're kind of surprised there is an arena in this tiny town. But your parents have talked about a cooperative between several towns, all of which can share the arena. There's no way Lakeside Bay could take up all the ice time.

After your mom parks the car, you haul your gear downstairs to unpack it. On second thought, you don't want Anna to do anything to your stuff, so you bring it all to the closet where Dad keeps his hunting equipment.

Back upstairs, you notice that your mom is on her phone. Her expression looks serious. *Uh, oh.*

"Hang on a second," she says into the phone. Then, to you, she asks, "Do you know anything about Anna's gear getting thrown into the showers?"

"Nope," you lie.

Your mom looks at you. You look down at the floor for the briefest of moments.

"Let me call you back." She hangs up, crosses her arms, and narrows her eyes. "I'll try again. Do you know what happened to Anna's gear?"

What will you choose to do?

To tell the truth, go to page 87.

To lie, go to page 97.

Hockey players don't just grab a random stick in a store like they're picking a jar of mayo. A hockey stick is like an arm to them. The flex, the way it lies, the tape job, the blade's curve—those are specific to each player.

You grab Ty's stick, as well as your own.

The team is still skating around the net on one half of the rink, all except for Ty. He's talking to the coach. No wonder he didn't make it back to the locker room. Is he telling Coach that Anna should play instead of you? If so, why this change of heart from the meanest guy on the team? Oh, no . . . does he have a crush on your sister? That would not be good.

Then again, maybe he doesn't have a crush on Anna. Is he telling the coach that she should be kicked off the team? You wish you could be a water bottle tucked next to the boards. You're dying to know what they're saying.

Just as you get close, they stop talking, and Ty turns away. He doesn't even look at you as he starts skating toward the gate.

"Ty," you say, "I have your stick."

He comes back and yanks it from your hand as he glares at you. Then he joins the others, skating around the net. He didn't even say thank you.

You head toward the net and chew up the ice. You go down into your splits, stretching a bit. The second before you're ready to take warm-up shots, a puck flies into your helmet cage. You see Ty smile as he goes for another puck. This time you're ready when he fires, and you catch it. Now, it's your turn to smile. Ty stares at you for a moment but then finds another puck. This time, he waits for his turn.

* * *

You're holding up okay as the game progresses, saving most of the shots against you. The only problem is that Anna keeps looking at you, her face wearing an angry frown. This makes you nervous, and the score starts to show it. You miss a shot in the five hole. Then, when one of the Buck forwards gets a breakaway, he flips it over your shoulder.

Ugh. The score is 0–2.

In the second period, Billy scores for the Blizzard.

Ten minutes later, the Bucks answer on a two-on-one breakaway. Despite how upset you feel, you have to admit that it was a nice play.

With eight seconds left in the period, Moose Creek scores again. You smack your stick against the ice. Your team goes into the second intermission, trailing by a score of 1–4.

Thankfully, the coach yells at everyone and not just you. "I don't care what the score is," he claims, which can't possibly be true. "You need to remember what we do in practice!"

The yelling doesn't seem to do any good. Moose Creek scores two more goals, back to back.

At the next whistle, the coach calls you to the bench. You skate to him, frustrated and tired.

"Bogue, you're out. Anderson, go in."

You look at Anna. She turns so red that she appears ready to explode. You feel like that, too.

Kohl gets scored on once, but at least Blake gets your team onto the scoreboard again, too.

After the game, with the final score of 2–7, the Blizzard bench is eerily quiet. Your team shakes hands with the Moose Creek players and then retreats to the locker room.

"Pathetic," Coach sneers. "It's like we've never even practiced. Maybe I'll get the little-kid drills for you to do tomorrow." He storms out of the locker room.

You need to do something to get better. And quick.

# 5

# Making Improvements

The team practice ended at 6:30. You're still at the arena, and it's 8:00. You got permission from the rink manager to stay late for some extra practice. Tonight, Billy is smacking puck after puck at you.

You've managed to stop a lot of his shots. If you can do the same thing during the games, you'll be a star.

Billy skates up to you, fast. Then he stops and his skates spray you with ice. "You're saving some nice shots, dude. But this isn't a game."

"Yeah, I know."

You weave your stick across the ice, as if it were a magic wand that could make you the greatest goalie ever to play.

"I'll keep coming to help if you want," he offers.

"That would be awesome," you say. "Thanks."

When your mom picks you and Billy up, she asks, "How did it go?"

"Good," you say. "But I still need more practice. I'm going to find out when I can come back again."

"Hm," Mom says. "Don't go too crazy, Adam. You've got to keep up with your homework."

"I know."

After she drops off Billy, you head for home.

"What's for dinner?" you ask. You're so hungry that you could eat your leg pads.

"Baked chicken and roasted sweet potatoes."

You practically start drooling.

As soon as your mom pulls into the garage, you run for the trunk to get out your pads and bag. She goes to the mailbox.

You get your gear unloaded as fast as you can and hurry to the kitchen. Your mom is there, holding a piece of paper and frowning.

"Adam," she says in a flat tone that tells you you're in trouble. "This is the quarter report card for you."

Uh, oh.

"You're not doing so hot," she continues.

"I'm not?"

"Is this a surprise to you?"

"Well . . . not really?" you stammer.

"How can you be getting a C in gym?"

"Probably test scores."

"You're also getting Cs in math and science. We have grade rules in this house. You'll bring up those three Cs or not play hockey."

"But science is hard."

"Get Anna to help you."

You groan.

"Your choice, Adam." She puts your report card on the counter and leaves.

Should you ask your sister for help with homework? Or will you see if you can do this on your own, without her help? What will you choose to do?

To ask Anna for help, go to page 64.

To work on your own, go to page 55.

**AWARD YOURSELF 1 SPEED POINT.**

**Go to page 50.**

AWARD YOURSELF 1 SKILL POINT.

**Go to page 50.**

Ty deserves it: You have to hide the stick. You grab his and put it in the same hand as yours. You walk out of the locker room. But just before you open the rink door, you open the side exit door and throw his stick into the snow. *Good luck finding that,* you think.

You pull the door shut as quickly as you can. Then you open the door to the rink—and you see why Ty's not coming back yet. He's talking to the coach.

Is he telling Coach that Anna should play instead of you? If so, why this change of heart from the meanest guy on the team? Oh, no . . . does he have a crush on your sister? That would not be good.

Then again, maybe he doesn't have a crush on Anna. Is he telling the coach that she should be kicked off the team? You wish you could be a water bottle tucked next to the boards. You're dying to know what they're saying.

You open the latch to the gate, let yourself onto the ice, and skate for the net. Ty skates back the way you came and heads for the locker room.

A few minutes later, you hear the rink gate slam open, and Ty skates onto the ice.

"Where's my stick?" he growls to the whole team.

"Duh," replies Keagan, "the locker room."

"It's not there," Ty barks.

"Maybe you forgot it at home," says Dominik.

"I'm not dumb. I know to bring my stick."

No one else says anything. They just keep shooting warm-up shots at you.

The buzzer rings, signaling game time.

"Where's my stick?" Ty yells.

"Play with an extra stick," Coach says. "We'll worry about your stick later."

You catch Ty's eye. He looks at you as coldly as the ice. "You went back to get your stick. What did you do with mine?"

You can't hold his stare. You suddenly feel guilty and a little afraid.

"See?" he shouts. "Adam did something to it!"

He starts skating toward you, but Coach is already there, next to him. He grabs Ty and pulls him toward the bench.

"Calm down, or you're not going to play," snaps the coach. "Pull yourself together."

You shake off your uneasiness and your guilt. You smack the pipes and get ready to play.

The game starts. Ty skates back and forth, looking for trouble—and he keeps looking at you. He looks like he's going to get himself a roughing penalty.

Not three minutes into the game, he does much worse than that. He flies into the crease and knocks a Moose Creek player into you from the side. You get hit so hard that you fall backward. Your head smacks against the ice.

When you wake up, you're lying in a hospital bed. A doctor is there with your parents.

"Hello," says the doctor. "Glad to see you're awake."

"Hey," you say, but it hurts to talk. It feels like someone has been hitting your head with a hammer.

The doctor says, "You're probably still in pain. You have a concussion. We're doing everything we can to make you feel better."

You try to nod, but that effort makes you feel sick to your stomach.

"What's worse, though," adds the doctor, "is the small crack in your skull."

Your eyes shift their focus to your mom. Her arms are crossed as if she's cold. Your dad's hands are on his hips. He stares at you like you're about to die.

"Your injury will heal," the doctor says, "but I'm afraid your hockey season is over."

**Go to the next page.**

# GAME OVER

**Try again.**

In the third period, you do stop Falcon from scoring any goals. Ty ties the game with five minutes left to play. You wish it had been Billy or Dominik or Blake. Anyone but Ty.

The period ends, and the game goes into overtime. Three minutes into it, Dominik gets sloppy with the puck. He loses it to a Falcon skater who charges toward you, alone on a breakaway. He crushes the puck past your shoulder. Goal. The Blizzard lose, 3–4.

The overtime loss seems to hit Coach hard. He rips your play in front of the whole team. "What were you doing out there? That was a complete lack of focus."

You just stare at the locker room floor.

Anna approaches you after Coach leaves. The last thing you want is to talk to her. But by looking at her face, you know that she isn't going to give you a hard time. She's probably feeling lucky that it wasn't her who stunk so much. But would she have given up four goals?

She pats your shoulder. "You played a good game."

"I let four shots go in."

"So? You stopped about 20 others."

You shrug. The coach wasn't impressed. You're not sure why she is.

**Go to page 44.**

You're tired of talking about this. Coach Wheeler, after all of these months, won't change his mind. You're sure of it.

"Mom, Dad, if you talk to the coach about Anna, I know what will happen. He'll just bench us both. That's the truth"

"He can't do that," your mom says.

"Sure, he can. He'll give a different excuse. He'll tell everyone that Kohl is a better goalie."

Your parents look at each other and shake their heads. But they don't argue. That means they believe you.

"Can you please just let it go, at least for now?" you ask. "We're almost done with the season. You guys can fight this over the summer."

"Yeah, okay," Mom says. "I suppose you're right. It just makes me sad for Anna." Tears form in her eyes.

"All we can do now," your dad says, "is hope your team gets to state—in spite of your coach."

"Right," you say, and then you take a bite of cereal.

**Go to the next page.**

The bad news is that you let in four goals against Hibbing. The good news is that the rest of your team steps up and puts in five goals—for a win! This means you're headed for the championship game tomorrow. If the Blizzard win, it will be the first time Lakeside Bay has ever advanced to the state tournament.

The entire team goes to watch a movie at the local theater. You feel like you're training for the Olympics when Coach says not to eat any candy or popcorn—and absolutely no soda.

After that, it's off to a restaurant for dinner. All the parents sit off to one side, while the players claim their space on the other side. The tables buzz with excitement for tomorrow's big game.

Your sister sits with your parents, though. When you see her with them instead of with the team, it smacks you in the head a little bit—you feel sorry for her.

Back at the hotel, everyone goes to their rooms to relax and unwind. Then it's time to sleep, but you're wired. You again have a hard time shutting off your brain. It makes for a very long night.

Tomorrow finally comes. In the locker room, Coach talks about your opponent: the Rice Lake Grizzlies. Again. This is going to be a tough game.

Indeed, it is. The Grizzlies score within the first five minutes. You don't panic. Your offense will tie it up.

But the Grizzlies score on you again when the center wraps around the net and sinks the puck before your pad can touch the post.

The first period ends. Coach is not happy.

In the second period, goal number three zooms over your glove. No one on the Blizzard seems to respond. It's like you've already lost. The team is fizzling.

You glance at the clock: only 11 seconds left in the period, and then you can get off the ice . . . and get yelled at by Coach.

But first, here comes the Grizzlies' center, flanked by the wings. The center passes to the left wing, who fires a shot at you. There's so much traffic that you can't see the puck—and when you hear the cheers, you know what happened. Now, you want to puke.

**Go to the next page.**

The score is 0–4. There's no coming back from that. It's finally time to admit it: Your sister is a better goalie than you are. Your team sure thinks so. You can tell by the way they've played for her—and by the way they haven't played for you. Is it time to speak up for her, to ask Coach to let her replace you? Or should you finish out the season? What will you choose to do?

To ask Coach to put her in, go to page 116.

To stay in the game, go to page 105.

You normally don't lie. You can't take the pressure. She'll find out, anyway, so the sooner, the better . . .

"Yeah, I do."

Her eyes widen. "What happened?"

You swallow hard. Then you quickly explain how Anna told you everything you did wrong after the game, and you got mad.

Your mom sighs, a deep and tired exhale. "Your coach, Dad, and I will talk about this. I'm not sure you should be allowed on the team anymore."

"Why? It's not like I do this every day," you protest.

"What happens if you get mad after every game? Are you going to throw your sister's—or another teammate's—gear in the shower?"

"Of course not."

"But it was okay to do it this time?"

"No," you mutter.

She puts her hand on your shoulder. "It's a good thing you told me right away, Adam, or you would've been in much more trouble."

**Go to the next page.**

When you and your parents meet with the coach, you're scared—*super* scared. You don't want to get kicked off the team.

"Here's what I think," the coach begins. "Adam competing against his sister is weighing on him. He sees how good she is, so he decided he had to show her who was boss. I don't condone it, but I get it. I grew up with three sisters, myself."

"And I have two," your mom says.

"So," Coach says, looking at you, "I think you need a consequence for what you did. But I won't kick you off the team. Is that okay with you folks?"

"Oh, yes, definitely," says your mom.

"From my end," says Coach, "he'll sit out this week. For Saturday's game, Kohl will start."

"Can't Anna start?" your mom asks.

"Not quite yet, but it's close." Your coach smiles at your parents.

You know he's lying. You almost roll your eyes.

"Sounds good," says your dad. "From our end, he's grounded for two weeks."

"And if any of her equipment is somehow ruined," your mom adds, "Adam will pay for it."

There goes your birthday money.

"I'm glad we got this sorted out," says Coach.

The coach leaves, but your parents want to talk some more. For a half hour, they discuss responsibility, sibling support, and honesty. When you finally go upstairs to your room, you thank your lucky stars that you didn't get kicked off your team.

# 7

# Birthday Surprises

Today is your birthday. Well, yours and Anna's. (She's older than you by six minutes.) Along with that good news, you also played a great game on Tuesday against the Moylan Muskies. You've always beaten them in the past. This time, the final score was 8–1.

You get to celebrate your birthday by trying to make it two wins in a row. Tonight, you play the Rice Lake Grizzlies. Unfortunately, you don't like your chances. While you always beat Moylan, Rice Lake is one of those teams that always beats you. A hockey loss would not be a very good birthday present.

However, your hopes take a turn for the better when you see their team during warm-ups. There should be about 16 players, but they only have eight. That's barely enough players for a team and not enough of them to have two shifts.

In the locker room, Coach Wheeler explains, "One of the boys had a birthday party a few days ago. A lot of the team went. The restaurant had some spoiled food, and all of them got really sick. They're still too weak to play tonight. A couple of the kids, in fact, are still in the hospital." He shakes his head. "We can beat this team tonight, although it's a bummer of a reason why."

"Coach," Alex asks, "why didn't they just forfeit?"

"I asked their coach the same thing," Coach replies. "He said they decided to consider it an intense practice." He smiles. "We can feel sorry for them, but we're not going to go easy on them. Let's go out there and give them an intense practice."

For the very first time in Blizzard-versus-Grizzlies history, the Blizzard win. The score, 7–3, doesn't reflect well on your team. Considering how short their bench was, you should have won, 10–0. In fact, Coach gives everyone an earful about not playing your finest, but you'll take the win.

The three shots they scored on you were some of the best plays you've seen. You're glad they didn't score even more goals with that kind of skill. You're also glad Anna didn't tell you how poorly she thinks you did.

With two wins in a row, the season is looking much better. The Blizzard's record is 9–5.

The arrival of the weekend means it's time for your party. Your mom picks up Hudson first. He has the widest shoulders in the class, and he's already been to nationals for wrestling. It's a good thing that you and Hudson have two classes together, or you'd never see each other with your different sports schedules.

"Hot caramel and chili, we're going to play laser tag!" Hudson exclaims.

"It's going to be so awesome," you add.

Your mom has rented the laser tag place for an hour, just for your party. When you arrive, you and your 12 guests get geared up in the glow-in-the-dark vests. Then you grab your lasers in the equipment room.

Just as you're about to head into the arena for the first 15-minute session, Ty and Keagan walk in.

"Weird," says Ty. "It looks like we weren't invited to the party."

"Nope," you say.

"But all my friends are here," Ty notes.

"Not your friends," says Billy. "Just teammates."

"Aw, my feelings are really hurt," Ty says. His voice drips with sarcasm.

"Come on," you say to your friends. "Let's go play."

"Bogue," Ty says, "I have an idea. Let me play in this first round. If I win, you tell Coach that Anna should play goalie in next weekend's tournament. If you win, I promise to be nice to you and your sister for the rest of the season."

Ty being nice? That's a tempting bet. But is it worth the risk? How many confidence points do you have?

If you have two or more points, go to page 123.

If you have one or fewer points, go to page 140.

"Okay, Zantana," you say to your sister, "let's go."

You tell your parents where you're going. Then you, Anna, and Ty grab your outdoor skates from your bags. Anna brings her pads, and you walk to the rink.

This is where it all started for you: an outdoor rink. Nothing feels better than the fresh air, the frozen ice, and a cold-swept sky full of stars. A dust of snow isn't bad, either, but full-sized snowflakes tend to make puck handling almost impossible.

Tonight is perfect—minus the dust of snow.

When you first started skating, you wanted to be a defenseman. You wanted to protect the net but also get to skate around—and sometimes score.

At those first pickup games, the teams went without goalies. The players just played. It was the best time to work on skating and stick-handling skills.

Tonight, Anna gets in the goal. You and Ty practice shot after shot at her. You offer her some tips, too—not that she needs them.

**Go to the next page.**

# 10

# Losing Big

You wake up on Saturday morning, feeling pumped about today's games. You and your parents leave Anna sleeping in the hotel room and go downstairs for breakfast. When you settle in at the table with two waffles, a bowl of cereal, and a banana, your parents look at each other and then at you.

"What?" you say.

Your mom replies, "We just need to talk with you."

You can't help but roll your eyes. You can guess what this is going to be about.

Dad chimes in. "Your mom and I feel that Anna is getting treated unfairly. *Still.* She's done well, both in practices and a game. But she's still not getting the ice time she deserves."

You swallow a bit of waffle. "She got to play in the North Tourney."

"Barely," your dad answers. "And only because the association required it. Listen, Adam, I know she's your backup, but she's your sister, too."

You dip another bit of waffle into a puddle of syrup. You know he's right, but you don't want him to be.

"We want to ask you again if it's okay to talk with Coach Wheeler about this," your mom says.

You move your cereal bowl onto your plate. You would love to be anywhere but here. You finally shrug.

"So that's a yes?" your dad asks.

"That's an 'I don't care.' I'm not sure my opinion even really means anything."

"It does," your dad says. "It's why we're asking."

Your opinion hasn't changed. If they talk to Coach, it will likely make things worse—for Anna and for you. Yet you feel stuck. Your parents will be disappointed in you if you refuse again. What will you choose to do?

To let them talk to Coach, go to page 132.

To refuse, go to page 83.

If your parents ever find out that you did it, you bet they will pull you off the team.

"Well?" your mom asks. "Do you know who soaked your sister's things?"

"Yeah . . . sort of."

"Explain."

"Mom . . . I really shouldn't."

"Oh, yes, you really *should*." She sounds almost ready to scream.

"Well, Keagan Osmund . . . it was him."

She spins away and grabs the hockey phone list.

Oh, no. She's going to call Keagan's mom. Then his mom will ask Keagan about it, and he'll deny it. Then what? You're not sure. You didn't think that far ahead.

"Hello, Katie? This is Lana Bogue. Do you have a minute? I need—"

The door opens. Anna steps inside. She's carrying a large, black, plastic bag.

"Sorry, Katie, can I call you back in a few minutes? My daughter just got home."

"Here's all my wet stuff." Anna drops everything by the door. Her eyes are red. She's been crying, but now she looks mad. "It's heavy, too. Thank goodness Chloe, Keely, and Mia helped me."

"Why not Avery?" you ask.

"She had to leave," Anna says. "How did you know she was there?"

"I saw you talking to them."

You immediately wish that you could take back those words. Your mom is practically Sherlock Holmes. You know what she's going to say next.

"You told me you didn't know where Anna was."

"Well, I didn't . . . uh . . . not the *whole* time."

"But you saw them talking after the game?"

"No . . . I mean, yes. I guess so."

Mom shakes her head. "I just about asked Keagan's mom if her son knew anything about Anna's gear. But I have a feeling you're not telling me the truth." She walks over and stands right in front of you. "Look at me."

Uh, oh.

"Did Keagan get Anna's equipment wet?"

You mumble, "No."

"Did he have anything at all to do with it?"

"No."

"So who put her things in the shower?"

Your shoulders droop. You close your eyes. "Me."

"You big creep!" Anna yells. "I can't believe you!"

"You teased me about the game," you protest.

"Because you stunk!"

"All right, that's enough," Mom says. "Anna, go put your stuff downstairs. Adam, go to your room. Your dad and I are going to talk with Coach Wheeler tomorrow. You're off the team."

"No, I'm not!" you yell.

"You don't get to make that decision. You made an extremely poor choice against your own teammate. Worse, it was against your own sister. You're done."

You run up the stairs and slam your bedroom door shut behind you. This is not how your hockey season was supposed to go.

**Go to page 81.**

In five minutes, Keagan has contributed to two goals for Duluth. He's definitely not doing his job. The coach must see that. But whether he does or doesn't, you have to say something.

"Coach?" You tell him. "Coach, Keagan isn't—"

"I know."

"Let me go in."

Coach Wheeler looks at the scoreboard. "Let me think about it," he says.

Well, at least that's something.

During the first intermission, the coach doesn't even stand. He sits on one of the benches, leans back, and closes his eyes. "I know I should be saying something right now that could motivate you, but I'm not sure what that is. This is the state championship, and unless you get your act together, we're going to lose."

He sits there another minute, apparently deep in thought. No one else says a word.

At last, Coach Wheeler stands. "Keagan, you're on the bench with me. Bogue, get some new pads. You're in on defense."

"What?" Keagan exclaims.

Coach Wheeler glares at him. "You are not playing like a member of this team, so you're off the ice. I don't know what you're doing, but I want to win this game."

Keagan throws his stick to the ground. Ty, who was sitting next to him, gets up and leaves the locker room. Anna just looks at you, wide-eyed. You jump up and start getting changed.

You manage to get out on the ice for the last part of warm-ups. You try not to think about this as the state championship. You pretend that it's a pickup game on the outdoor rink. You're just having fun with your friends, that's all.

You provide a bit of a spark for your team. Blake puts the Blizzard on the board with a goal, thanks in part to a great steal by you.

The rest of the period is filled with plenty of back-and-forth action, but neither team manages a score. You head into the next intermission, trailing 2–1.

In the locker room, Coach Wheeler is pumped up. You've never seen him like this.

"This is it, you guys! This is it! We're only down by one, and you're finally playing like you're supposed to. Now get out there and win this thing!"

Anna smiles ever so briefly.

As the third period begins, Duluth scores another quick goal, but your team doesn't lose its confidence. On the contrary, except for Keagan, everyone on the bench sits up straight, eagerly watching every move and smacking the boards with their sticks whenever something good happens.

Dalton skates behind the net, sneaks to the other side and knocks the puck into the Tempest's net. It's a beautiful wraparound goal, and it puts the score at 2–3. This game's not over, yet.

The very next time down the ice, Elijah intercepts a Tempest pass and streaks toward the goal. There's no one between him and the goalie. He has a breakaway. You've never seen him skate so quickly. Elijah lifts his stick and slaps the puck toward the net.

Score!

The Blizzard fans jump to their feet. The Blizzard bench is rocking. Even Keagan is on his feet now. The game is tied.

Two minutes later, the Tempest center gets a breakaway of his own. He charges toward Anna.

Oh, no, this could be trouble.

Anna comes out to challenge him. She plays him perfectly, and his shot soars over the net.

No one sits down. The arena vibrates with cheers.

You glance at the clock. Only 1:27 to go.

Alex has the puck behind the Blizzard net. You're with him, and Billy skates around as the team regroups on your side of the ice.

Alex passes the puck to you, and you skate up the side of the rink, just like you've done a million times at the outdoor rink. You pass to Dominik.

He's pressured and passes back to you. You slide the puck over to Billy, who passes it to Blake. The puck goes back to Alex, who controls it and passes it back to you.

There's a lot of traffic between you and the goalie, but you have a clear look at the net. You can take the shot and try to score, or you can risk a pass to Billy. He's closer to the net, but can you get the puck to him?

You take a deep breath. This moment is going to take everything you have—everything you've worked so hard to become.

Add together all of your points.

If you have 12 or more points, go to page 153.

If you have 11 or fewer points, go to page 142.

"I'm sorry, Anna, but I'm really wiped out."

"Seriously? It was one game today."

"Yeah, but it was a good game. It went into OT."

Anna rolls her eyes. "For one minute!"

"I played a good game. I'm tired. Okay?"

She doesn't say another word. She just storms away, leaving you to feel like the bad guy. You walk back to your hotel room, still feeling a bit guilty. But Anna is your competition. And you really are tired.

Nevertheless, you kind of wish you had gone. An outdoor rink is where hockey started for you. Nothing feels better than the fresh air, the frozen ice, and a cold-swept sky full of stars. A dust of snow isn't bad, either, but full-sized snowflakes tend to make puck handling almost impossible.

You remember when you first started skating. You wanted to be a defenseman. You wanted to protect the net but also get to skate around—and sometimes score.

At those first pickup games, the teams went without goalies. The players just played. It was the best time to work on skating and stick-handling skills.

Oh, well, you're here now. You might as well relax and try to get some much needed sleep.

**Go to page 95.**

You've never heard the locker room so quiet. Coach doesn't even say a word. He keeps shaking his head. Then he finally leaves.

"Step it up, you guys!" Ty yells, cracking the silence. "We're better than this!" He points his stick at you. "And you, Bogue, start minding the net. In case you didn't know, we'll go to state if we win."

You stare him down. He finally breaks his gaze and storms out of the locker room.

Early in the third period, Ty's frustration turns into a goal. Elijah smacks one in, too, from back near the blue line.

But the clock keeps ticking, not that the time really matters. The Grizzlies score two more times before the clock hits zero.

The game ends, 6–2, and so does your season.

**Go to page 81.**

You just lost, and the last thing you want to think about is giving up your position. "No," you say. "It won't work. And maybe you should try supporting *both* of your children." You walk away before they can reply.

You hear your dad say, "No, let him go."

You're glad that you planned a sleepover at Billy's house tonight. You don't have to deal with your parents anymore—at least, not until tomorrow.

As you look for Billy, you find your sister instead. She's with Mia, Avery, Chloe, and Keely again.

She barely looks at you as she says, "I could've saved those shots."

You ignore her and keep walking.

When you catch up with Billy, you load your stuff in the back of his family's van. Then you climb into the backseat. *Please don't talk to me. Please don't talk to me.*

"Sorry about the loss," Mrs. VonRuden says.

"Thanks," you reply.

"Yeah, bummer," says Mr. VonRuden.

*Please don't ask about Anna.*

"You know," says Mrs. VonRuden, "I haven't seen Anna in a game, yet. Have you?" she asks her husband.

"Nope. She hasn't played. Right, Adam?"

"No," you agree.

Billy says, "Kohl hasn't been in much, either."

You kick him in the shin.

"We've noticed," says Mr. VonRuden.

Billy leans over and whispers, "What? I got them off the topic of Anna."

You shake your head.

Billy's parents don't ask any more questions on the drive back to Lakeside Bay.

At breakfast, Billy's parents bring up Anna again.

"Don't take this the wrong way," Mrs. VonRuden says, "but Anna should get to play. There's no girls' team, so it would be fair if she did play this season."

"It doesn't work that way," you answer. "If one goalie is better, that goalie plays."

Billy's parents look at each other.

"I've been to some practices," Mr. VonRuden says. "Anna is a good goalie. I'm not saying she's better than you. I won't get into who's better than whom. But she's good enough. I don't know why Coach Wheeler won't play her."

You stifle a sigh. As politely as you can, you tell them, "I'd rather not talk about it. It's been tough living with my backup."

**Go to the next page.**

When you get home, Anna is in the living room, working on her science homework. Of course, you have this homework, too. You grab your backpack from your bedroom and return to the living room.

"I'm not helping you," Anna says.

"I didn't ask for help."

"You didn't now, but it'll be the same answer later."

You frown. "Why do you have to tease me about how smart you are?"

"Why won't you convince the coach to play me?"

"Not my decision," you tell her.

"Baloney," she retorts.

"Anna, Coach doesn't care what I think."

"But you could say something!"

You don't reply. You simply retreat back to your bedroom. You find it harder than ever to focus on your homework. Instead, you can't stop thinking, *Maybe, just maybe, she's right.*

# 8

# North District Tournament

December and January pass by in a blur of birthdays, holidays, regular games, tournaments, and homework. You still haven't talked to your parents again about Anna getting into a game. They haven't talked to you, either, which surprises you.

The Blizzard enter the North District Tournament with a record of 17–10. Your first opponent is the Cass Rams, a team with a record of 18–9.

You skate out to the crease and chew up the ice. When you're done, you notice Coach inching along the ice, toward you. A long time ago, he skated in a semi-pro hockey league. He might have made it to the National Hockey League, except he tore up his knee. He's been coaching ever since.

"Bogue, change of plans: You're out of the game."

"What? Why?"

He sighs. "I have to get your sister on the ice."

"But I thought—"

"Yeah, well, it's not my call. I've been told it's time."

"By who? Not my parents."

Coach Wheeler doesn't answer. He just looks at you.

"The association?" you ask.

"We had several meetings," Coach tells you. "This is the decision. The deal is I only need to play her for two periods. You can come back in for the third."

Your sister skates in to take your place. You follow Coach Wheeler to the bench. You look at the bleachers, but you turn away before you see your parents.

Even though you've already chewed up the crease, Anna repeats what you've done. Ugh! You can't watch her either. You look at the Rams' goalie, instead.

You tell yourself to buck up and deal with this. The association made a decision, and there's nothing you can do about it, except keep a positive attitude.

The game begins, and Anna dominates. You're not sure if that makes you feel better or worse. She stops shots that you might have missed. She catches every puck like it's a softball. She doesn't even flinch against the hard shots.

At the end of the first period, the Blizzard are ahead, 2–0. By the end of the second period, it's 4–0.

Coach looks at you. "I did what I promised. Let me know if you want to play the third."

If Anna plays this whole game, your team will start to wonder who's in the net next time. Then they'll start to doubt you. You can't let that happen. On the other hand, Anna has a shutout going. Maybe you should stay out of it and let her have this chance to shine. What will you choose to do?

To agree to play, go to page 115.

To stay on the bench, go to page 146.

Knowing Coach Wheeler, he's probably thinking about pulling Anna already. If you talk to him, you'll just be giving him an excuse to do so. Instead, it's your duty to tell your sister—your teammate—what she's doing wrong so that she can get better.

She starts toward the door, but you call her name. She looks back at you, a frown on her face that's so strong it almost glows.

"Just wait a minute," you say.

She exhales and moves over to let the other players out. She stands next to the door, the frown still on her face—maybe a deeper frown now.

"You let two goals in so far."

She shakes off a glove and reaches up to pull out her mouth guard. "Thanks for the reminder that—"

"Let me talk for a sec," you say.

She's a statue.

"You're not coming out of the crease, Anna. You've got to challenge those shooters. You're giving them more net to look at—"

"I know."

"Well, then, start doing something about it."

She glares at you. "Done?"

"Just go back to playing how you play. Go back to how you got us this far."

Her frown relaxes a bit.

"You're an unreal goalie, Anna. You're better than I am, okay? You can do this."

**AWARD YOURSELF 1 TEAMWORK POINT.**

You're glad that you said something. Now, Anna is definitely coming out of the crease. She's stopping shots that otherwise could've gone in.

The problem isn't Anna, anymore. It's the offense. The Blizzard are still at zero goals. The offense needs to step it up—and now.

Well, there's one other problem, too: Keagan is still out there, trying to make Anna look bad. She's saving the shots, but he's not helping her one bit. In fact, his "mistakes" are setting up goal opportunities for the other team. You wonder if anyone else has noticed.

You get your answer in the locker room after the second period.

"Keagan," the coach says, "start playing defense out there, instead of wrestling. Understand?"

"What?" Keagan plays dumb.

Coach looks at Anna. "I don't know what happened, but you're doing much better. Keep it up." Then he chews out the offense for five minutes.

With about 15 minutes left in the game, you start getting nervous. If your team can get that first goal, it could really jump start things.

You look at Anna. She's doing well.

You look at Keagan. He's still not playing defense for Anna. You have to wonder: Why doesn't Ty say anything to his friend? You don't get it, but it's making you really mad.

One thing's for sure: Keagan needs to come out of this game. But who can replace him? Well, *you* know the ins and outs of defense. Should you talk to Coach about it? Coach Wheeler is so stubborn that, if you say something, he might just leave Keagan in to prove you wrong. In that case, is it better to wait for Coach to make up his own mind? What will you choose to do?

To talk to Coach, go to page 134.

To wait and see, go to page 144.

"Yeah, I'm in, Coach," you tell him.

You play the entire third period, but all you manage to do is ruin the shutout. A girl—maybe someone in the same dilemma as Anna—scores on you. Her shot is high, but the roar of the crowd tells you that it didn't fly over the net; it smacked into it.

The Blizzard still get a win. But you leave knowing that your sister played better than you.

Your team goes to Pizza Ranch for the buffet. You hear Ty tell Keagan that he doesn't understand why you're eating since you didn't do anything. You just walk away.

**Go to page 147.**

You've never heard the locker room so quiet. Coach doesn't even say a word. He keeps shaking his head. Then he finally leaves.

Although you're ticked off and want to prove that you can mind the net, you know what's best for the team—and for your sister.

You follow Coach out the door. You find him at the end of the hallway, talking to the assistant coach.

"Coach," you say. "I don't want to do this, but . . . you need to put Anna in. She's better than me. She's better than Kohl. If there's any chance to win the game, you need to put her in."

He doesn't say anything.

"Look, the worst thing that happens is we still lose. But maybe she'll spark the team. Maybe . . . I don't know. Maybe we can still do this."

He stares at you for a moment. Then he slowly nods. "Okay, Bogue, I suppose it's worth a shot."

The team heads onto the ice together, and you watch as Coach tells Anna the news. Her face lights up, but then her expression morphs into one of determination.

You watch your teammates as they spot *her* going to the net instead of you. Their necks grow taller. Their backs get straighter. Their legs move faster. You can feel the new energy that Anna has created.

Suddenly, you're sure: the Blizzard are going to win.

Ty scores the first goal. Still down by three. Elijah smacks one into the net from the blue line. Now, you're only down by two.

On the other end of the ice, Anna makes save after save. There's no way the Grizzlies are going to score again. So all the team needs is two more goals.

Billy scores on a breakaway with eight minutes left. That brings the score to 3–4. The Grizzlies are scared. They look panicked. Their fans do, too. All the noise is now coming from your side of the arena.

Anna continues to make brilliant saves, even though her defense makes a few mistakes in front of her. With less than four minutes to play, Ty fires a shot at the net. The goalie is in position to block it, but Dalton puts out his stick and taps the puck, changing its direction just enough . . . Goal!

Tied, 4–4. Unbelievable.

As the last two minutes wind down, the action stays on the Grizzlies' side of the ice. Anna practically doesn't need to be out there. Your teammates pass the puck back and forth. The Grizzlies can't catch up to it.

Ty and Billy get off a couple of shots. The goalie blocks them, but the puck always bounces back to a new Blizzard player.

With 32 seconds left, Alex slams a slap shot, which clangs the pipe, and the puck goes in!

Time has never moved more slowly as you watch the last half-minute from the bench. When the clock finally runs down to zero, everyone on the team mobs Anna. The Lakeside Bay Blizzard are on the way to state!

# 11

# Going to State

For the next few days, before the state quarterfinals, Anna is relentless. She wants you to keep shooting at her at the outdoor rink. The coach has agreed to let her start, so she wants to get as much practice as possible. By Tuesday, she's practically invited the whole Blizzard team to practice with her.

Although you've known all week that she's going to play in the net, you can't help but think that something is off. You really want to be in that net. But she is, and there's nothing you can do about it.

When game time comes, you stand at the side of the bench and watch your sister. Although you feel useless right now, you believe that the extra practice did her some good.

She makes incredible saves throughout the game. In fact, she's probably the MVP. The Blizzard win by a score of 4–1. Next, it's on to the semifinals.

* * *

As you open your eyes, Anna is walking to the hotel room door, then to the window and back again. Ten minutes later, she's still moving.

"Anna, go get breakfast or something. Or take a run around the hotel, like, 200 times."

"Easy for you to say."

You prop yourself up. "Excuse me?"

She doesn't stop moving. "Sorry, that's not what I meant. I'm just nervous about today's game, okay?"

You flop back down on the bed. This is going to be an interesting day.

Three minutes into the state semifinal game, the center for the Waseca Edge shoots a high blocker and scores. It's not a good way for the Blizzard to start.

As time keeps ticking away, you notice that Anna isn't coming out of the crease to challenge the shooters. She usually does the opposite, acting just like she's a brick wall, almost daring someone to score. But her nerves are probably making her tuck into the crease, as if her body wants to block the entire net at once, which it definitely can't do.

You want to yell, "Hey, goalie, get out of there a bit and challenge those shooters!"

A few minutes later, Waseca scores again.

You notice something else, too. At least, you think you do: Whenever Keagan is on the ice, he's not really defending his goal very hard. He's being physical, so it looks like he's doing his job, but he's not stick handling and checking the way he's supposed to. Does he *want* to lose or what?

At the first intermission, the Edge are still up, 2–0.

In the locker room, each time Coach Wheeler says a word, he hits his fist into his hand. "This. Is. Not. The. Way. We. Play!" He rubs his temples. "This is state. This is the time to show everyone out there what you got! Let's go, you guys!" He settles into a quick glare at Anna before he leaves the locker room.

**Go to the next page.**

If the Blizzard are going to have any chance of winning, your goalie needs to start challenging the shooters. Should you tell Anna and try to get her to adjust? It might make a big difference—or she might not listen to you. Or should you tell Coach what the problem is, so you can get out there and try to win the game? What will you choose to do?

To talk to Anna, go to page 112.

To talk to Coach, go to page 128.

"Sure," you tell Ty. "Let's go."

Ty gets his gear on, while you and the others get a look at the landscape. There are two floors, a couple of ramps, and lots of neon pillars. The object of the game is to tag opponents with your laser.

Ty and Keagan come into the room.

"Ready," Ty says.

"Don't you want to look around?" Keagan asks.

"No, I've been here before." He smiles.

An employee comes through the doorway and asks if the teams are ready.

"Yep," you say.

"Then . . . begin!"

The lights go out, and objects start to glow.

You run for cover, peek out, and fire at Ty. You know that you've tagged him when his vest flashes. He runs, and you try to follow him. He jumps out from behind a pillar and surprises you.

Something in your gear yells, "Warning! Warning!" so you know he fired but barely missed you.

For the next 14 minutes, you run around and tag each other, try to dodge the infrared beams, and listen to the sounds of the lasers firing. You feel sweat in your armpits, down your back, and on your forehead.

You sure hope that you're beating Ty.

The lights go on after 15 minutes. You walk back to where the others are.

"How'd you do?" asks Hudson.

"Don't know," you say. "I think I got him a lot, but he got me, too."

The employee points to a TV screen. "These are where the results will post."

You wait for what seems like forever. Then . . .

**Team Ty:** score: 9,300 | accuracy 46%
**Team Adam:** score 10,200 | accuracy 39%

Nobody says anything.

"Now what?" Connor finally asks.

"Higher accuracy, of course," Keagan replies.

"Yeah, right" Hudson says. "Adam got a better score."

You tell Ty, "I guess we'll have to let the goalie thing sort itself out."

"You're just a chicken, Bogue," Ty says. "You're afraid Anna is better than you."

"I'm doing fine, Selver. Our record isn't bad."

"It's not great, either. At this rate, we may not make it into Regions at the end of the season. So remember *that* when you're watching your sister outplay you in practice." He turns to his friend. "Come on, Keagan."

They walk out together.

You wonder, *What does Anna see in that guy?*

**AWARD YOURSELF 1 SPEED POINT.**

The Blizzard enter the weekend tournament with a record of 11–5. You get off to a great start, winning the first and second games. However, Saturday afternoon pits you against the very healthy Grizzlies. They put up nine goals against you. Your team only scores once.

The loss earns you a place in Sunday's third-place matchup versus the Wabedo Ice Wolves. Their star player, Eric Lincoln, is well known in the hockey world.

The first period is a shutout for both teams, but you let in four goals in the second period. Three of them come from Lincoln.

During the intermission, Coach asks three times, "What are we doing out there?"

Nobody answers.

In the third period, Dalton scores once. But neither team scores again. That means . . .

Fourth place.

Your parents are waiting for you after the game.

"Sorry about the loss, honey," your mom says.

"Thanks."

Dad chimes in. "So . . . your mom and I have been talking, and we think you look good out there. But we're starting to believe that Anna's not being treated fairly."

You roll your eyes at them. "Do we have to talk about this right now?"

"Yes," your mom says. "We need to talk to Coach about this, too."

"Aww, Mom . . ."

"Last week," your dad says, "I watched the practices from upstairs."

"You did?"

He nods. "Anna is good."

"I know."

"You're good, too, Adam," he says. "That's why your team has won a lot of its games. But Anna should get a chance to play. It's not her fault there's no girls' team."

You cross your arms. "Why are you telling me this? It's not up to me who plays and who doesn't. But I guess it's nice to know you think she's better than me!"

"Adam," your mom says calmly, "that's not our point at all. Of course, we want you to play. We want *both* of our children to play. But it's not even about who gets to play and who doesn't. It's about Anna being treated in a certain way, just because she's a girl."

"We want what's best for Anna," adds your dad. "But we won't go behind your back to do it. You're just as important to us as she is. That's why we're talking to you. We'll only talk to Coach about getting her on the ice if you give us the okay."

"What do you think, Adam?" asks your mom.

This is a disaster. How can you say no to them? Of course, the problem is that you know Coach Wheeler. This sort of "talk" with Mom and Dad isn't going to work on him. In fact, it'll only make him mad. Anna won't get to play—and you'll probably end up on the bench next to her.

Still, maybe it's worth a try. Should you allow your parents to talk to Coach? Or should you tell them not to do it? What will you choose to do?

To let them talk to Coach, go to page 132.

To tell them, "No," go to page 106.

It's your obligation to tell your coach that Anna is doing the wrong thing. Winning this and going to the state championship is on the line. You're a goalie, the one who's spent the most time on the ice this season. You need to be out there.

You follow Coach through the lobby, down the hall, and into the bench area beside the ice. You look out to see the other players warming up on the ice, while Anna roughs up the crease.

"Coach," you say, "Anna isn't doing what she needs to do out there. She's not challenging the shooters. We'll lose if she keeps this up. I want in."

Coach Wheeler watches the players. He finally looks at you. "If you think you can do better—"

"Yes, I definitely can. I've been watching Waseca's offense, and I can do this. Please, let me go in."

"Okay, Bogue. But if we lose, it's on you."

No pressure.

You skate over to your sister. "Sorry, Anna, Coach wants you out. He's putting me in."

"Why?"

"Because you're not challenging the shooters. You're giving them more net to aim for. You're too nervous."

"I . . . but . . ." She turns away from you and skates toward the bench. She unlatches the gate and kicks it open. She goes into the farthest corner she can, away from the ice.

You can't think about her now. You finish cutting the ice and take some warm-up shots from the other guys. You're ready.

You manage to keep the puck out of the net, and you celebrate when, finally, Billy scores.

After a second intermission, you know that your team has a chance. You're only down by one—and your team can tie or even win this game, as long as you don't let the Edge score.

However, a shot does make it past your glove side. Then another goes through the five hole. You want to melt into the ice and disappear.

When the final score shows Waseca: 4 and Lakeside Bay: 2, all that you can do is stand and stare at the red lights that display the loss. Your ears fill with the Edge's yells and whoops.

Most of your teammates skate by you, tap you on the shoulder, and say, "Good job." Ty and Keagan skate past you without even a glance in your direction. Anna does, too. You thought that you could help your team win this game. You were wrong.

**Go to page 81.**

The question really isn't if you're going to say something. The question is why bother? Coach Wheeler gets to make the decisions. You're better off by keeping your mouth shut.

Just then, you hear Coach shout, "Osmund!"

When Keagan skates to the bench, the coach yells, "Sit down! That's the worst defense I've ever seen. Do you see the goalie in the white uniform? That's your goalie. Guys in red? The opponent. Got it?"

Keagan doesn't reply.

During the first intermission, the coach doesn't even stand. He sits on one of the benches, leans back, and closes his eyes. "I know I should be saying something right now that could motivate you, but I'm not sure what that is. This is the state championship, and unless you get your act together, we're going to lose."

Coach lets Keagan back in for the second period. At least, now, he's not making his errors as obvious, but you've seen him in enough games to know that he's still not helping Anna the way he should be.

One goal slips past her top shelf because Keagan didn't stop the wing. Another goal goes in when he's on the bench. You can't blame him for that one. Anna just didn't get her stick down fast enough.

The Blizzard head into the second intermission down by a score of 0–4.

"Now would be the time to score," is all that Coach Wheeler says.

But it seems as if the Blizzard players have given up. The third period wears on. And on.

Anna lets one more shot go in. The Blizzard offense never finds the net. The Duluth Tempest win, 5–0, and your team is left trying to celebrate second place. You might feel proud of what turned out to be a successful season, if you weren't so mad at yourself for not doing more about Keagan.

**Go to page 81.**

Even if you tell your parents, "No," you don't think they will listen. Besides, it's probably the right thing to do. You only hope that you're wrong about how the coach will react.

"Okay, fine," you mutter. "Talk to Coach Wheeler, and see what happens."

Your mom smiles. "Oh, good," she says. "We'll do that right now. Thank you, Adam."

Your parents hurry away. So many different thoughts swirl in your head—it's like several players are shooting pucks at you, all at once.

You go and get ready to leave. On the way, you cross paths with Anna. She must not know your parents' plan. She doesn't even look at you.

* * *

In the locker room, Coach Wheeler gathers the team to talk about your next opponent. "If you play the way we practice, we can beat them," Coach says. "Now get out there and warm up."

As the others leave, Coach announces, "Adam, Anna, Kohl, hang on a sec."

You three stay until everyone else is gone.

"Apparently, there's some complaints about the way I'm coaching. Now, I realize I've been making some bad decisions about who's playing goalie. In light of all that, Kohl is our goalie from here on out."

You look at Kohl. His jaw drops.

"But Coach, I—" Anna begins.

"Kohl has proven himself at practice, so it's his turn to start."

"Coach Wheeler, if my—" you start to say.

"That's all," Coach snaps. He leaves the locker room.

"I'm sorry, guys," Kohl says. He follows the coach.

You and Anna look at each other, too shocked to speak. Now, at least, you know how she feels. You'll be watching the rest of the season from the bench.

**Go to page 81.**

You can't just sit back and watch the game go down this way. The team carries extra pads, and you can throw them on in a heartbeat after all the years of practice.

When the next whistle blows, you approach your coach. "I want to go in and play defense."

Coach Wheeler looks at you, his face puzzled.

"Keagan is messing with Anna. He doesn't care if we win or lose. He just wants to make her look bad. She's going to get scored on any minute, and I used to play defense when—"

"Keagan wouldn't do that. Besides, look at the score. I'm worried about getting on the board right now, not our defense."

The whistle blows, and the game continues. You look at the clock: 13:08.

**AWARD YOURSELF 1 CONFIDENCE POINT.**

When the whistle blows again, you once more ask, "Coach, can I—"

"No."

You sigh and move back to the end of the bench. Before you get there, your teammates stand and start to cheer. You look over to see a huddled celebration with Dominik in the middle. You glance up at the scoreboard and see a "1" tick onto the screen.

The Blizzard are only down, 2–1.

The goal seems to send electric vibes through the bench—and it energizes your team.

When Billy gets onto the ice, he blasts in a shot from the corner, and it scoots past the goalie. You somehow manage to jump up and down in your big, thick pads. The Blizzard can win this!

With three minutes left on the clock, Dalton finishes the rally. He serves the goalie a five-hole shot that skids through his legs and into the net.

Blizzard: 3, Edge: 2.

"Timeout," shouts Coach Wheeler.

When Anna comes to the bench, she takes off her gloves and grabs a water bottle.

"How're you doing?" you whisper to her, as the coach talks to the team.

"More nervous than before."

"Yeah, but it doesn't show. You're doing great."

"Thanks."

"You got this, Zantana."

She looks at you. "Thanks, bro."

Waseca skates furiously, grueling and desperate. They attack the net, time and again. Keagan seems to let them—even help them. But Anna saves every shot.

The Blizzard count down the last five seconds. Then everyone rushes over to congratulate the goalie.

Lakeside Bay is going to the championship!

# 12

# The Big Game

Anna is pacing again.

"Seriously, go run around the hotel," you snap.

"And risk getting hurt?"

"Well, at least I'd get to play, then," you joke.

She smiles. "Then I'm definitely not running."

Although you're bummed that you probably won't be playing the first time Lakeside Bay goes to state, you're still excited about your team. And, yes, you must admit that you're proud of your sister, too.

The championship game starts at 1 p.m., plenty of time for Anna to grow more nervous. The Blizzard will play the Duluth Tempest, the team that also took home the championship last year. They're undefeated, and no one (outside of your team) thinks you can beat them.

Now, you feel nervous for Anna.

The morning goes by slowly . . . so, so slowly. After what seems like *days* pass, your team comes together in the locker room.

"Yep," the coach says, "this team won state last year. But you earned the trip to be here, so I expect you all to play like you belong here, too."

During the first five minutes, the Blizzard players seem too nervous, even scared: sloppy passes, out-of-control skating, poor decisions. Anna makes some good saves, but she seems unsteady, too. She's going to let a goal slip by if she doesn't get her act together.

And Keagan is at it again.

You should have talked to him last night. But you didn't. You still don't really understand why he's not defending his own goal. He's always been a bully, but you never realized he had something against Anna. Why would he jeopardize a state championship?

You watch Keagan pretend not to see the Tempest wing who skates beside the net—a perfect position to get a pass and score. Instead, Keagan glides away and covers a defenseman.

The Tempest center passes it to the wing, who scoops the puck into the net. Goal.

You close your eyes and take a breath. Your coach must have seen that. But Keagan stays in the game.

Two minutes later, the Tempest center charges at your goal with the puck. Keagan is in his path—but instead of stopping the center, he skates toward the wing, as if the center will pass it.

The center shoots, and the puck speeds by Anna's outstretched glove hand. Just like that, the Blizzard are down, 0–2.

Keagan needs to come out of the game—and fast. Do you dare talk to Coach about it yet? Will he think you're good enough to replace Keagan? Add together your talent, speed and skill points. How many points do you have?

If you have five or more points, go to page 100.

If you have four or fewer points, go to page 130.

"No, thanks," you tell Ty. "I'd rather just hang out with my friends today."

He shakes his head. "Whatever. You're afraid because you know I'll beat you."

You shrug. "Go ahead and think that. I'm here to have fun. I'm not interested in making a bet with you."

He keeps tossing out insults, but when you and your friends walk away, he takes the hint and leaves.

You and the others go into the play area and get a look at the landscape. There are two floors, a couple of ramps, and lots of neon pillars. The object of the game is to tag opponents with your laser.

An employee comes through the doorway and asks if the teams are ready.

"Yep," you say.

"Then . . . begin!"

The lights go out, and objects start to glow.

You run for cover, peek out, and fire. For the next several minutes, you and your friends run around and tag each other, try to dodge the infrared beams, and listen to the sounds of the lasers firing. You feel sweat in your armpits, down your back, and on your forehead.

It's a wonderful way to celebrate your birthday with friends, and you're glad that Ty didn't stick around long enough to ruin it.

* * *

The Blizzard enter the weekend tournament with a record of 11–5. You get off to a great start, winning the first and second games. However, Saturday afternoon pits you against the very healthy Grizzlies. They put up nine goals against you. Your team only scores once.

The loss earns you a place in Sunday's third-place matchup versus the Wabedo Ice Wolves. Their star player, Eric Lincoln, is well known in the hockey world.

The first period is a shutout for both teams, but you let in four goals in the second period. Three of them come from Lincoln.

During the intermission, Coach asks three times, "What are we doing out there?"

Nobody answers.

In the third period, Dalton scores once. But neither team scores again. That means . . .

Fourth place.

**Go to page 126.**

Billy can score. He's been doing it all season. He's been doing it since you were Mini Mites. But you have the puck, and you're ready. You've practiced slap shots all of your life, during pickup games at the outdoor rink. This is your chance to redeem yourself for getting benched. This is your chance to become the star of the entire season.

You hit the puck with all of your might.

It soars toward the net. It looks like the most perfect, the most beautiful shot you've ever hit . . .

*Doink!*

. . . until it hits the pipe on the side of the goal and ricochets back into play.

You stand there for a moment, staring into the net. How could you have missed that shot?

You barely notice as a Tempest player controls the puck. He passes it to a teammate, who zips by you.

Oh, no! You should've gotten back on defense.

He glides into the open, and all you can do is chase him. You watch helplessly as he fakes to his right.

Anna falls for it and slides out of position.

The Tempest player scoots to his left, pulls back his stick, and fires it forward, hitting the puck and sending it toward the open side of the net.

Goal.

With 46 seconds to go, the Blizzard try to rally—but there just isn't time. In the end, your team is left trying to celebrate second place. You might feel proud of what turned out to be a successful season, if you weren't so mad at yourself for making such a boneheaded play.

**Go to page 81.**

You can't talk to Coach about this. He won't believe you, and there's no way he'll put you into the game if you haven't even practiced on defense. All you can do, for now, is just sit back and watch the game.

You look at the clock: 13:08. Then you sigh and move to the end of the bench.

Before you get there, your teammates stand and start to cheer. You look over to see a huddled celebration with Dominik in the middle. You glance up at the scoreboard and see a "1" tick onto the screen.

The Blizzard are only down, 2–1.

The goal seems to send electric vibes through the bench—and it energizes your team.

When Billy gets onto the ice, he blasts in a shot from the corner, and it scoots past the goalie. You somehow manage to jump up and down in your big, thick pads. The Blizzard can win this!

With three minutes left on the clock, Dalton finishes the rally. He serves the goalie a five-hole shot that skids through his legs and into the net. Blizzard: 3, Edge: 2.

"Timeout," shouts Coach Wheeler.

When Anna comes to the bench, she takes off her gloves and grabs a water bottle.

"How're you doing?" you whisper to her, as the coach talks to the team.

“More nervous than before.”

“Yeah, but it doesn’t show. You’re doing great.”

“Thanks.”

“You got this, Zantana.”

She looks at you. “Thanks, bro.”

Waseca skates furiously, grueling and desperate. They attack the net, time and again. Keagan seems to let them—even help them. But Anna saves every shot.

The Blizzard count down the last five seconds. Then everyone rushes over to congratulate the goalie.

Lakeside Bay is going to the championship!

**Go to page 137.**

"Coach," you say, "I think you should let Anna play this out." You swallow. Hard. "She's earned it."

**AWARD YOURSELF 1 TEAMWORK POINT.**

The game ends with the same score: 4–0. It's a shutout for Anna. You're glad the team won. You're less than glad about not playing in a game for maybe the first time ever. That rattles you.

After beating the Rams, your team heads to Pizza Ranch for the buffet. You hear Ty tell Keagan that he doesn't understand why you're eating since you didn't do anything. You just walk away.

**Go to the next page.**

The next morning, the Blizzard play the Thief River Falls Whiteout, a team with a tough reputation. As the rest of the team heads to the ice, Coach Wheeler keeps you, Anna, and Kohl in the locker room.

"Okay, Adam, you're in." Coach starts walking out.

"What?" Anna says. "After how I played last night?"

"Yep," is all he says before leaving.

"What's going on?" Anna says.

Kohl shrugs.

You mumble, "I don't know," as you stand and walk out of the locker room.

Although the Whiteout are indeed a tough team, you do your best to show the coach you belong in the net. Throughout the game, you let three goals slip in—one for each period. But the Blizzard wings match each one. The Blizzard win after Blake scores the team's fourth goal with 2:35 left in the game.

You're elated.

Anna doesn't say a word.

The championship game is against the Wabedo Ice Wolves, a team that beat the Blizzard earlier this season. Now, it's time for a revenge win.

As you chew up the ice, you keep chanting in your head: *You can do this. You can do this.* Even if you let in a shot or two, you can save the rest and hope your team scores. You've got to prove to your teammates that you deserve to be out here more than Anna.

In the first period, the Ice Wolves come out strong. Eric Lincoln scores twice. Your team doesn't match them. In the second period, however, the Blizzard shake things up with three straight goals.

The Ice Wolves score again in the third, and the game is tied, 3–3. You have a love/hate relationship with ties. You love the adrenaline, but you hate the pressure. Your mom always says that she can't stand these tight games. You get it; you'd much rather be up by six.

With only 1:27 left in the game, Dominik manages a sweet steal. He smacks the puck toward the Ice Wolves' goal. It hits the pipe and ricochets into the net.

That's the game winner. The Lakeside Bay Blizzard are tournament champions!

# 9

# Helping Anna

At school, you can barely concentrate. You're super excited that the Blizzard won the North District Tournament. Now, the team might be good enough to win the Regions Tournament. (If you do, you'll be on your way to the State Tournament.) The first game is Friday against the Moylan Muskies.

Thursday night, you lie in bed and just stare at the ceiling. You're so nervous that you can hardly close your eyes. You run plays in your head, over and over. You're not sure what time you finally drift to sleep, but the last time you look at your clock, it reads 1:06 a.m.

Friday morning, awkward silence rides with your family in the car to Grand Rapids. Your mom and dad talk a little. Mom even sings a little and moves her hands likes she's dancing, which you think is a little bit crazy. Other than that, a solid brick wall might as well exist between you and Anna. You try to focus on the landscape outside your window, rather than the bad vibes she's sending your way.

The Muskies have definitely improved this season. They even score first, a hard slap shot from the blue line. Unreal. Ty gets the Blizzard your first goal, and about five minutes later, Alex scores a goal, too.

Between periods, Coach Wheeler asks, "Did you all leave your brains at home?"

No one answers.

In the second period, you make two of your best saves ever: one with total pressure around the net. But the Muskies are relentless, and they score again. The game is tied, 2–2.

Billy gets a beautiful goal from Dalton's drop pass, and the Blizzard head into the third period up by one.

Right after the face-off, the Blizzard defense gets caught out of position, and a Moylan forward zooms toward you. He shoots through your five hole—and scores: 3–3. You smack your stick on the ice. *Come on, Adam!* you yell in your head.

Eight minutes later, the period ends, still tied.

That means "sudden death" overtime. If you aren't the next team to score, you lose—and your season is over. You *really* can't mess up now.

Coach Wheeler draws some new plays on the white-board above the bench. "Come on," he says when he's done. "We beat this team before. Finish the game."

"One, two, three, Blizzard!" you all yell together.

You try to remember everything any coach has ever told you about being a goalie. You try to remember the best saves and the best games you've ever played.

Fortunately, your teammates hardly need you. After only 52 seconds, Elijah gets a breakaway. He takes off toward the Muskies' goal, and you watch as he shoots one into the top shelf.

*Goal!*

You finally exhale.

**Go to the next page.**

That night, at the pool, Anna pulls you and Ty aside. "There's an outdoor rink just a block from here," she says. "Can you two come with me and help me get some extra practice? Since Coach played me last weekend, maybe he will again."

You and Ty look at each other. Then you focus back on Anna. Do you want to help her? She is your sister, after all. Of course, if she gets much better, she really will take your position from you. Plus, you're pretty tired and need to rest.

How many teamwork points do you have?

If you have four or more points, go to page 94.

If you have three or fewer points, go to page 104.

Billy can score. He's been doing it all season. He's been doing it since you were Mini Mites. But you have the puck, and you're ready. You've practiced slap shots all of your life, during pickup games at the outdoor rink. This is your chance to redeem yourself for getting benched. This is your chance to become the star of the entire season.

Except this game isn't about you. It's about your team. Billy is in better position than you are. It'll take a great pass, but if you do this right, he'll be shooting at an open net.

You scoot to your right, and the goalie shuffles with you. You pull back your stick, as if you're going to fire a shot at the net, and the goalie crouches low—just like you wanted him to.

Instead of knocking the puck toward the goal, you slide it between two defenders, directly to the front of Billy's stick.

The goalie is too far to his left now. He can't recover in time. Billy flips the puck forward, and it splashes into the back of the net.

Goal!

With 46 seconds left, the Tempest try to rally—but there just isn't time. They glance upward, time and again, watching the seconds tick down.

*Three . . .*

*Two . . .*

*One . . .*

You shout for joy. You drop your stick and throw your gloves into the air. You skate in circles, watching your teammates laugh and scream and cry. Someone leaps onto your back, and you fall to the ice.

"I love you, Adam," her voice says.

You've done it. Your sister has done it. Your team has done it. The Lakeside Bay Blizzard are state champions!

# Epilogue

Anna is on fire. Well, not actually, but she might as well be. It's a typical summer day, drenched in humidity with the sun blazing. Nevertheless, Anna has to wear all the goalie pads as she practices on Rollerblades with you and your friends. You know what it's like for her; you know how much she's sweating beneath it all.

You, on the other hand, no longer wear goalie pads. You get to wear the regular pads of a player at defense. Permanently. Hockey season will return again in a few short months. You can hardly wait. You, Anna, and the Blizzard will be ready to defend your championship.

**Go to the next page.**

# YOU WIN

**Congratulations!**

# CHOOSE TO WIN!

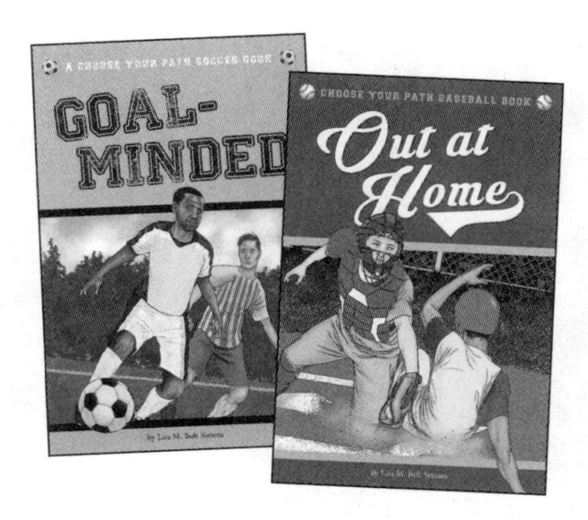


Read the fast-paced, action-packed stories. Make the right choices. Find your way to the "winning" ending!

*Goal-Minded*
*Out at Home*
*Save the Season!*

---

YOU'RE THE MAIN CHARACTER. YOU MAKE THE CHOICES.

# CAN YOU SURVIVE?

*20,000 Leagues Under the Sea*
*Adventures of Perseus*
*Adventures of Sherlock Holmes*
*Call of the Wild*
*Dracula*
*King Solomon's Mines*
*Merry Adventures of Robin Hood*
*Three Musketeers*
*Treasure Island*
*Twelve Labors of Hercules*

# About the Author

Lisa M. Bolt Simons has been a teacher for more than 20 years, and she's been a writer for as long as she can remember. She has written more than 20 nonfiction children's books, as well as a history book, *Faribault Woolen Mill: Loomed in the Land of Lakes*, and she is currently working on several other projects. Both her nonfiction and fiction works have been recognized with various accolades.

In her spare time, Lisa loves to read and to scrapbook. Originally from Colorado, Lisa currently lives in Minnesota with her husband, Dave, and she's the mom of twins, Jeri and Anthony. She was a busy sports mom for over a decade.

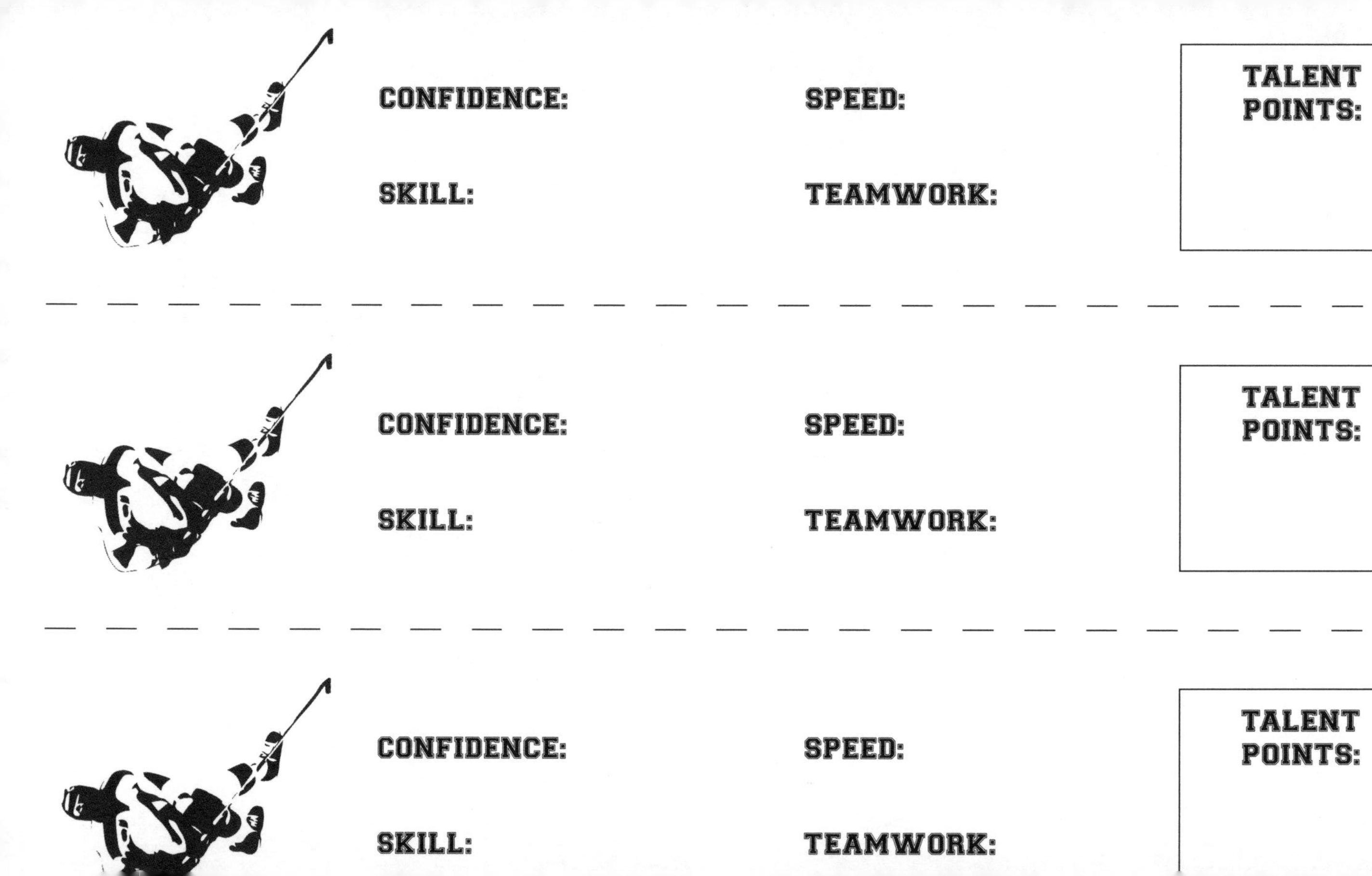
CONFIDENCE:
SPEED:
SKILL:
TEAMWORK:
TALENT POINTS:
CONFIDENCE:
SPEED:
SKILL:
TEAMWORK:
TALENT POINTS:
CONFIDENCE:
SPEED:
SKILL:
TEAMWORK:
TALENT POINTS: